FINAL NOTICE

A Novella

ALLISON SPEKA

Skylar

I HAD BEEN BENJAMIN MEAD'S EXECUTIVE ASSISTANT FOR three years now, and for two of them I'd been in love with him.

Okay, maybe it was actually more like two years, fifty-one weeks, and four days. But I had denied my feelings for so long that I had even convinced myself that I felt nothing for him in that first year.

I strolled into the office a little past eight and set down a cup of coffee on my boss's desk like I did every other morning. Typically, I tried to arrive at least an hour before Ben so I could get everything organized for the day.

Sighing, I powered on my computer and smiled at the sticky note stuck there.

Stop getting in so early, you're making me look bad :)

It was part of our ritual. Ben and I always left little notes for each other.

The phone rang and I reached over to answer it, surprised to be getting any calls this early.

"Hello, Benjamin Mead's desk."

"Skylar, it's Melanie."

I winced, already dreading whatever bomb she was about to drop on me. Melanie was head of the company's public relations team. Ben and his partner Nathan Shaw founded the dating app, Pulse, in their college dorm room almost eight years ago. It was now used by millions worldwide. Lately, the application and the company had been in some hot water due to Ben's playboy ways consistently making the tabloids.

"Ben was caught in some hot water the other night and it's finally coming to light," Melanie continued.

"How bad is it?" I asked, my heart dropping. It was bad enough harboring feelings for Ben, but it made it even more painful when I was the one that had to do damage control for the messes he continued to get into.

"Pretty bad. You know the Smith sisters?"

"From the reality TV show?"

"That's the one. He got caught two timing them."

I groaned. Maybe my naivety was to blame for falling for a guy riddled with so many major red flags, but when it came down to it, no one knew Ben like I did. He showed me his softer sides. He'd been vulnerable with me. Maybe it would never amount to anything, but the torch I carried for him still burned brightly even as I cleaned up mess after mess.

Melanie continued to rattle off details of the current predicament as I took notes.

"Got it, I'll send you a copy of his statement once I have a chance to speak with him," I told her.

Melanie snorted: "Why wait? You know you'll be the one writing the statement anyhow."

"I still need to get his approval."

She sighed. "Send it once he's in. We need to get on top of this fast."

I hung up and started to type out a sample of what he should say. I included the typical apology as well as complimenting the sisters on their entrepreneurial smarts. Ben would glance at it and approve it like he always did.

"Morning, Sky." My heart melted at the sound of my nickname on his lips. He was the only one that called me that. Typically, I hated having my name short-ened, but the way he said it made me feel special.

"Morning," I said. "Your breakfast is already at your desk."

"You're the best." He dropped a coffee on my desk. "Here's your midmorning pick-me-up."

I smiled and took the latte appreciatively. Even though I was the one that should be getting him a latte, we had our routine down. He knew I finished my first cup of coffee on my commute here and always brought one to tide me over.

"Thanks, Ben."

He nodded and smiled before brushing into his office.

The door had barely closed behind him when a tall

man dressed casually in jeans and a T-shirt blew by my desk. Nathan Shaw didn't even glance down at me as he passed. Sometimes he gave me a curt hello, but that was only when he was feeling extra friendly. For two founders, the two men could not be more different. While Ben was charming and sociable—maybe overly sociable— Nathan was stoic and showed no emotion. He was even too much of a control freak to have his own assistant. I had tried to hire one for him, but he scared off anyone that deigned to try and take over some of his menial tasks.

Even after working here for three years, Nathan still intimidated me.

"What the hell!" I heard him bark as he slammed Ben's door behind him.

I could hear muted yelling as the two of them went at it. I was sure Nathan had been informed of Ben's latest indiscretion. Nathan ran on logic and hard work. It drove him mad that Ben could let his trivial playboy ways consistently make bad press for their company. It didn't help that they had recently sold a portion of their shares to investors and now had a conservative board to answer to.

The door opened and Ben stuck out his head. "Sky, can you come in here for a minute."

"Of course." I popped out of my seat and followed him to his office. He towered over my petite five-foot-one frame—although most people did. Any time we were near each other, I couldn't help but breathe in his intoxicating scent and think how nicely I could tuck myself under his arm.

"Sky, can you assure Nathan here that damage control is already being done for the misunderstanding with the Smith sisters."

"Misunderstanding!" Nathan exclaimed. "You were sleeping with one sister and then went out with the other. You were both photographed half naked, all over each other at the bar last night."

Ben sighed. "What an invasion of privacy."

Nathan's eyes narrowed. "Why can't you just keep it in your pants for five godamn seconds?"

I cringed and looked at the carpeted floor. You would think hearing all this would dump a bucket of ice water over me. How could I possibly be in love with such a player that treated women like that? Alas, my heart clearly had a mind of its own, and apparently according to it, all could be forgiven when it came to Ben.

"I already spoke with Melanie. She's ready to make a statement across all your socials. I've drafted one for you if you want to take a look before I send it out."

"Nah, I trust you." Ben winked at me and it sickened me that it gave me butterflies. He turned back to Nathan. "See? It's all taken care of. You need to stop worrying."

"You're going to cause me to go gray early," he mumbled.

Ben clapped a hand on his shoulder. "Always so dramatic."

Nathan stormed out of the office leaving just Ben and me.

He shot me a sheepish look. "Sorry you're always having to cover for me like this."

"It's no problem," I said, forcing a smile.

"I'm sure you'd rather be just about anyone else's assistant but mine."

"Don't be ridiculous. I love working for you."

He reached out and ruffled my hair. I hated how much I craved the little sign of affection. He used to hand them out more freely, but after the incident at the holiday party a few months ago, Ben had become more distant with me. And I hated it.

"I don't know what I'd do without you, Sky."

I grinned up at him. "Well good thing you never have to find out."

He looked at me and I swore I saw sadness in his eyes.

I returned to my desk and spent the rest of the day doing damage control.

———

"GOODNIGHT, BEN. I'LL SEE YOU ON MONDAY." I POKED my head into his office. I always liked to say goodnight, partly to see him one more time before I left for the evening and partly to make sure he didn't need anything before I headed out.

"See ya," he said, not looking up from his computer. I tried not to let his lackluster goodbye get to me as I walked out of our office and into the warm San Diego air.

I had moved here three years ago from Kansas City and I would never get sick of this weather.

As I walked home, I tried not to let the events of today weigh on me too heavily. Still, cleaning up yet another mess for Ben that involved other women stung.

Most would think I'm nuts for harboring these feelings, but most people weren't privy to one important fact.

At the holiday party exactly two months and twenty-five days ago, Benjamin Mead kissed me. And I'm not talking a polite peck—he really kissed me. The kind where we were both clawing at each other as if we couldn't possibly get close enough.

I flashed back to the memory.

Ben had been having a hard evening. He grew up in a very wealthy family that only cared about image and money. He had opened up to me about it in the past. That night, his father had showed up at the party uninvited and basically called him a fraud. Said he would never amount to anything without the family name.

I had found Ben in the garden outside the party, mulling over the words.

"You okay?" I had asked, sitting down on the bench next to him.

"I'll never be good enough for him."

I shook my head. "He's an asshole. You can't waste your life trying to please him. Look at everything you've built." I gestured to the room inside where hundreds of employees were celebrating Pulse's record-breaking year. "We're all here because of you. You're a success, Ben. Whether he sees it or not is his problem."

Ben sighed and stared at me. "How do you always know the right thing to say?"

"Um, because it's my job," I said, playfully nudging his shoulder. The two of us were always flirty. Sometimes, I thought maybe it was crossing a line, but mostly I was just happy to be able to touch him every once in a while.

"Is that all it is?" Ben asked, his brow furrowed.

I tilted my head, puzzled by his intensity. "Well, no. I actually believe everything I say to you. You really are amazing."

He shook his head. "You're amazing too, Sky. I don't know why you bother being my assistant. You're way too smart for this."

Because I couldn't stand the thought of not seeing you every day, I think but don't say out loud.

I licked my lips, suddenly all too aware of his proximity. "I love being your assistant," I finally said.

"I wouldn't know what I'd do without you," he said, not breaking his stare.

"You would be just fine. You're the most capable man I know. You're smart, you're kind, you're—"

"Stop," he said.

"W-what?" My voice came out shaky.

His gaze bore into me. "You can't go saying all those nice things while wearing that pretty dress."

"I can't?"

"No." He leaned in even closer. "You're making it entirely impossible not to kiss you."

I gasped at his admittance. In all my months of

harboring unrequited feelings, I had never imagined Ben would actually say something like that.

My mouth parted slightly as I sat there speechless.

Ben groaned. "Don't look at me like that, Sky."

"Like what?"

"Like you want me to kiss you."

I swallowed. "But I do."

He cursed under his breath and I thought for sure he'd move away. But instead, he brought his hand to the back of my neck. Before I could think twice, he leaned in and pressed his lips to mine. The softest of kisses sent an immediate tingling sensation through my entire body. I reached my hands around his neck and grabbed on, pressing my mouth to his with more need. A sound like a growl erupted in his throat. My mouth parted and he slipped his tongue in, hungrily exploring me. I had never felt need like this—like I would absolutely combust if he didn't touch every inch of me. He reached down and grabbed my leg, swinging it up so it was on his lap. Now pressed against him, our kiss became even more desperate. The amount of pleasure I felt just from his lips on mine was astounding, I couldn't imagine what he would do if he had the rest of me.

"Fuck, Sky," he said against my lips. "I've wanted to do this for so long."

"Me too," I admitted, but I could barely get the words out because his lips covered mine as he deepened our kiss.

Feeling bold, I took my hands away from his hair and used them to push myself up off the bench.

Leaning into my other leg that was on his lap, I let my body fall so that I was straddling him. He grabbed my upper thighs and scooted me up against him so that I could feel his hard length beneath his pants. I placed my hands on his chest and pressed my hips into his as our kiss became more frenzied. He moaned at the friction I caused.

Voices trickled out from the party as someone opened the door to the garden. As they neared, Ben grabbed my leg and tore it away from him, placing me back on the other side of the bench. His breathing was labored. I just sat there in a daze, still stunned that had actually happened.

I shook the memory from my mind as I approached my apartment.

The front door to my building slammed shut as my two next door neighbors rushed out screaming at each other. I ducked out of the way as they barreled past me, nearly knocking me into the hedges.

"I can't believe you texted her back," Stella said.

"I can't believe you'd go through my phone!" Stanley yelled back.

"I'm staying at my sister's!" she screamed, running down the block.

"Good! Don't bother coming back!"

They ran off down the street. I grabbed the door before it swung shut and climbed the small flight of stairs to my apartment. My building wasn't luxury by any means. Paint chipped walls and flickering lights greeted me every day, but it was home. Plus, I could walk to work at an affordable price, which really sold me on the place.

I swung open the door to find my roommate, Bria, lounging on the sofa with big headphones on. When she spotted me, she waved and took them off.

"Stella and Stanley were in full force out there," I said, peeling my shoes off and collapsing on our worn armchair.

"Thank god they finally took it outside," Bria said. "They've been at it for the past hour. I could hear every word of that fight through these paper-thin walls. Is it rude if I go over there with cookies and kindly point out that they make each other miserable and should break up?"

I laughed at her suggestion. "I'll help with the baking, but I'm not getting involved in their feud."

Our neighbors weren't really named Stella and Stanley. We had coined the nicknames because of the constant screaming matches we could hear through our shared wall. Although we hadn't officially met, I felt I knew them intimately considering I could recite a laundry list of their issues.

"So how was work?" Bria asked, tossing the bag of chips in her hands.

I caught it and reached my hand into the bag. "Oh, you know, the usual. Cleaning up another scandal for the one and only Benjamin Mead."

Bria groaned. "Again? You've really got to quit that job."

"You know why I can't," I muttered, stuffing a

handful of chips into my mouth. I usually turned to comfort food after an especially tough day.

Bria sighed and shook her head. "No, I know of exactly one good reason why you definitely need to quit."

I ignored her, having heard this lecture before. Bria was my first friend here. I had answered her *roommate wanted* ad. After three years, we had traded apartments but remained roommates. She was well aware of my feelings for Ben and was the only person I had told about our kiss. To say she found me delusional would be an understatement.

"I can't just leave him," I finally said.

She huffed and sunk down into the couch, feigning exhaustion from this conversation. "You can't just stay either. I see how down you are. Ever since that kiss, you've got this false sense of hope."

"No I don't," I lied.

"And it tears you down every time you have to deal with the fallout of his philandering ways."

I stuffed more chips into my mouth to avoid responding.

Bria jumped up and grabbed my arm. "Come on, let's go out and shake the awful stench of this day."

I let her drag me off the chair. All I felt like doing was curling up on the couch and watching a rom com, but I knew Bria would pester me until I gave in.

"Let me at least take a shower."

BRIA GIGGLED AS WE STUMBLED THROUGH OUR FRONT door. She had dragged us to some trendy new bar and forced me to flirt with any guy that caught her eye. She told me it was therapy to get over Ben. While I had been resistant at first, after the second gin and tonic, I managed to find some fun in the evening.

"I hope you got the second guy's number," Bria said, heading straight for the kitchen to grab a glass of water.

"Not my type," I insisted, going to my room and slipping on sweats.

Loud moaning and a thudding sound came from next door.

"Guess Stanley and Stella made up again."

The thudding grew louder and I covered my ears. While I wasn't a total prude, listening to other sexual escapades made me uncomfortable to say the least. Plus, the sounds coming from that room sounded barely human. My high school boyfriend certainly had never elicited such sounds from me.

"We've got to move," I said, reaching into my bag and pulling out my phone. The two missed calls caught my attention. Both Ben. I checked my text messages.

> Ben: Sky, you there? Can you come over?

> Ben: Please pick up.

> Ben: I really need you.

I was already up, rushing back to my room to change.

"What?" Bria asked, leaning on my door frame.

"Ben just texted. He said he needs me."

I rifled through my closet.

"Skylar!" she exclaimed, a look of horror on her face. "It's past midnight. You can't go over there."

"He texted me like three times. It must be important." I thought back to the only other time he had texted me this late. It was just a few nights before our kiss. When I arrived at his house, he was sipping whiskey. He had just had a particularly challenging conversation with his father. He told me he couldn't stand being alone. When he reached for his phone, he had realized mine was the only voice he wanted to hear.

So yes, maybe I was delusional for loving Ben. But between a statement like that and the best kiss of my life, could you blame me? It wasn't like he gave me zero to go off of.

Bria threw herself in front of my closet. "I forbid you from going."

I glared at her. "You aren't stopping me."

She shook her head in disappointment. "Fine. But I refuse to let you change. He doesn't deserve a cute outfit. Plus, you don't want to look desperate."

"Fine," I relented, moving out of the room. "Don't wait up."

"Be careful," Bria warned.

———

THE CAB PULLED UP TO BEN'S LARGE TOWNHOME. I GOT out of the car and hurried up the front walk. The first time I had seen his place, I had to pick my jaw up off the floor. The place towered three stories tall and had a grand staircase nearly the size of my whole apartment building.

I reached the front door and knocked.

"Come in." Ben's voice sounded panicked.

As soon as he saw me, relief took over his face. "You came."

"Of course. What's going on..." My voice trailed off as a stunning, scantily clad blonde stormed into the room.

"Who the hell is this?" she demanded. "If this is your PR person, tell her she's too late. I'm calling the paparazzi."

I recognized the woman immediately as Sandra Smith. After all, I had been doing damage control on the story of Ben cheating on her with her sister all afternoon.

I shot a confused look at Ben, who met me with pleading eyes.

"This is my assistant Skylar Evans."

Sandra glared at me. "Get lost, Skylar. There's nothing you can do or say to keep me from throwing this asshole under the bus and running over him." Her hard gaze cracked as a sob escaped her throat before she ran out of the room.

"What's going on?" I whispered "Is this about earlier? I know you two-timed her but I thought the worst of it was over."

Ben ran a hand down his face, looking exhausted. "It is—well, was."

"Explain," I demanded, irritated all my hard work to

handle this situation might have been for nothing. After releasing my perfectly crafted statement and calling the magazines, I had selected gifts for both Smith sisters and sent them along with an apologetic card signed by Ben.

"She just showed up here and now she won't leave." Ben threw his hand in her direction. "She threatened to call the paparazzi and make a scene. I can't have that. The board is already breathing down my neck."

I narrowed my eyes. Something didn't add up.

"Why would she just show up here and threaten to make a scene out of nowhere? According to her social media story, she was over you."

Ben looked at the floor sheepishly. "She might have come over to thank me for the gift I sent."

"You mean the one *I* sent," I corrected. Dread filled my chest at the direction this conversation was headed.

"Right." He nodded. "Well, the thanking turned pretty physical if you know what I mean. Anyway, after we finished, I asked her to leave and now she's freaking out."

My heart cracked in two at his admission. He didn't need me here to talk. He needed me to clean up yet another scandal.

"So you slept with her after cheating on her with her sister, tried to kick her out, and now she's upset?" I deadpanned, ignoring the fire burning behind my eyes.

He balked at my dirty look. He was used to my sweet demeanor, but he was about to find out I could only be pushed so far.

"It sounds worse when you say it like that."

"I'm out of here." I tried to push past him, but he

stepped in front of me. He grabbed my arms and crouched down to meet my gaze. *Damn it.* I hated how I couldn't turn away from him. Even as tears threatened to burst free at any minute.

"Please. Sky," he said. "I need you. I can't fuck up again."

I searched his eyes, numbness overtaking me. "Fine. I'll talk to her."

"Thank you so much."

I didn't stick around to hear his praise. I walked through the house until I found Sandra curled up on a bench, crying.

She lifted her head up when she saw me. "I thought he really liked me," she sniffed.

I can relate to that.

"He has that way about him," I said in a comforting voice. "Charming but flighty. You can't take this personally. Ben will never settle down."

The advice I gave to her was just as much for her benefit as it was for my own.

"I hate that he made me fall for him."

"Amen, sister," I muttered.

"Huh?" She looked at me with mascara rimmed eyes.

"Look," I said, placing a hand on her shoulder. "Sure, you could cause a scene and hurt his reputation, but he's not worth it. Do you really want your name dragged through the tabloids any more than it already has been today?"

She shook her head.

"Exactly. You're better than this. You're Sandra

freaking Smith. Men want you and women envy you. Forget Ben and move on with your life."

She smiled. "You're sweet and you're right." She stood, wiping her eyes. "I'm out of here." She paused at the doorway. "I don't know how Ben landed such a sweet assistant, but get out before he breaks you."

"Too late," I muttered, brushing my eye to catch an escaped tear.

I heard Sandra's footsteps echo and the front door slam closed. I remained frozen on the bench for a moment.

Ben rounded the corner, looking relieved. "You did it. I can't believe it. I've been trying to get her to leave for hours."

"I can't believe you," I said, staring blankly ahead.

"Huh?" He tilted his head, looking at me with a puzzled expression.

"You've got a lot of nerve." I shot up off the bench. "You called me over here to get rid of your one-night stand. What's the matter with you?"

Ben ran a hand through his tussled hair and paced the room. "I'm so sorry. I never would have under normal circumstances. But you know the pressure I'm under."

"The pressure you put *yourself* under."

"That's fair."

"I'm so out of here," I grumbled, pushing past him.

"Sky!" he called, following me. "I'm sorry, okay? I'm an idiot. It's just you're always the first person I think to call."

I glared at him, thinking how that sentence might have once caused my heart to soar.

"I think it's time you find a different person for that."

"What do you mean?" His brow knit with concern.

"I mean, I can't do this anymore." A few tears ran down my cheeks.

"Sky..." Ben's expression became pained. "I never meant to upset you like this. I'm so, so sorry. I won't call you like this ever again."

"Did I ever mean anything to you?" I whispered.

Ben tilted his head "What? You're the best assistant—"

"No," I cut him off. "Did I ever *mean* anything to you? Because when you kissed me, I thought I might."

He tossed his head back and groaned. That single sound sliced the rest of the way through my already fragile heart.

"I never should have done that. I knew you'd think too much of that kiss. I thought if I never brought it up again, we could pretend it never happened."

My tears fell freely now. "I could never pretend."

Ben grabbed my hands. I felt too numb to pull them away.

"I'm such a mess, Sky. You deserve the world, not the crumbs I could offer you. Please don't let that moment ruin us."

"I'm done," I repeated, calmly removing my hands before walking toward the front door.

"What?" Ben asked, following me.

I sucked in a breath, urging my raging heart to slow down. From the doorway, I turned back. "Consider this my notice. In exactly two weeks—fourteen days—I'll be moving on."

"You can't do that. You just—I can't—"

I ignored Ben's flustered objections.

"Goodnight, Ben."

With that, I closed the door on his shocked face.

Ben

I PACED THE FRONT ENTRYWAY OF MY HOUSE FOR WHAT felt like the hundredth time. Shock and anger still ripped through me at Skylar's departing words.

Consider this my notice.

Like hell I would! I needed her. Rage simmered in my gut at the thought of losing her. Had I pushed her too far tonight? Maybe. But it wasn't my fault. I was in hot water with the board and getting that situation sorted out was an emergency. No one could handle an emergency like Skylar. And she has spent all afternoon helping me untangle myself from my current web of drama. How was I to know she would snap this evening?

Because she's in love with you, asshole.

I shook the intrusive thought from my mind and walked over to the bar to pour myself a tall tumbler of whiskey. I knocked it back in one gulp and winced. Skylar had been working with me for the past three years, and I couldn't deny I noticed that she probably felt something for me. Between our flirtatious banter and her always eager to do things off the clock for me, I knew she saw me as more than a boss.

But besides the fact that she was excellent at her job, she was also a fantastic listener. I couldn't talk to anyone the way that I could talk to her.

Fuck.

I should never have kissed her at the holiday party. That moment had sent this situation spiraling out of control. I knew I didn't deserve her and had no business laying any sort of claim on her. But I couldn't help it. My desires won out in that moment. Ever since she started working for me, my thoughts toward her had been less than pure.

She was just so innocent and kind. I couldn't get enough of her. I constantly pushed my boundaries as her boss, yet I couldn't resist.

Skylar wasn't the type of girl a guy could screw and leave. She needed and deserved more than I could ever give to her. So even though I had a moment of weakness and kissed her, I had held her at an arm's length ever since.

I came from a wealthy family and loneliness had followed me since childhood. My parents and siblings were distant, only ever meeting to discuss money or image. None of us cared about each other. My family was likely the reason I slept around and had never had a meaningful relationship in my entire life. And let's be real, my parents were definitely the reason I didn't believe in marriage. They had cheated on each other ever since I could remember. They barely bothered to be discreet about it.

I'd worked hard to distance myself from my family name. No one could say I had things handed to me. I built this company with Nathan and I never took a cent of my parent's money to do it. Now my net worth was double theirs.

I still remembered Sky's first day of work. She was a fresh arrival in town and she stuck out like a sore thumb. Her clothes were all wrong and she was too sweet. She had been such a bright spot in my life since that day. Which was why I couldn't let my indiscretion sour our relationship, because like I said, I needed her. Apparently, all that effort I had put into avoiding her had all been for nothing because in the end I had managed to fuck it up in an epic way.

Her heartbroken face flashed through my mind as I knocked back another whiskey.

Did I ever mean anything to you?

She would never know how much she meant to me. Hell, *I* wasn't even sure how much she meant to me. If the pain cutting through me at her departure was any indication, I felt a hell of a lot stronger than I cared to admit.

A pounding on my door caused my heart to practically leap out of my chest. My hope that it was Skylar returning to talk things through dissipated almost immediately when I took note of the sheer force behind the knock. That definitely wasn't Skylar.

I yanked open the door to find my partner, Nathan, glowering at me.

"It's one a.m. Can you please tell me why the hell I just got a call from Melanie freaking out that you're about to ruin your reputation once and for all?" He barged in, shoving me in the process.

Shit. I might have called her when Sandra had first started threatening to call the paparazzi. She hadn't answered and I'd left an anxious voicemail.

"It's taken care of," I said.

Nathan threw his hands in the air looking pissed. "There should be nothing to take care of!"

I felt bad, Nathan was typically the picture of stoicism. It wasn't easy to ruffle his feathers, but I had become an expert at it these past few years. If there was one thing Nathan Shaw cared about, it was work. And unfortunately for him, my behavior had put our leadership and our company under a microscope lately.

"Look, I'm sorry Melanie called you and got you all worked up but it's handled. I handled it." Well, Skylar handled it right before she shook up my entire world. Should losing an assistant feel like my heart was just ripped out of my chest?

"I'm so fucking sick of this, Ben." Nathan pulled out a glass and poured himself something at my bar. "I just want this company to succeed and it seems like you're hellbent on making that difficult."

"It's already a success," I pointed out. "We've sold part of it for millions. We're rich, Nathan."

"As if money is all that matters," he scoffed.

I shrugged. "I mean it definitely has its perks.

"You're impossible," he muttered, sipping his drink.

I should tell him that the board had been

discussing forcing us to merge with a company with a better reputation, but I didn't want to anger him further. Nathan usually avoided board meetings at all costs so I could be selective with what I decided to share.

"I know," I admitted. "But hey, it's over now for real. Skylar came over here and cleaned everything up. I won't make the mistake of sleeping with a Smith sister again."

Nathan laughed bitterly. "Like that was the only mistake." He lifted his glass. "Thank god for Skylar. She's an expert at dealing with you."

The sound of her name caused me to clench my hands into fists. "She just gave her notice," I finally said aloud.

"I'm not surprised," Nathan said in an infuriatingly calm voice. "You put her through too much. It was only a matter of time."

"I don't put her through too much," I argued. Even though my gut reaction was defensiveness, I knew he was right. I pushed her and now she would be gone. "I can't lose her," I muttered.

"Then you shouldn't have asked too much of her."

"I know." I groaned running my hands over my face.

"Maybe you could give her a raise," he suggested. "God knows she deserves it."

"I don't think it's quite that easy," I said thinking about our kiss for the thousandth time since it had happened. "I-I think she has feelings for me."

Nathan shook his head. "Are you sure?"

The pain in her eyes haunted me. "Pretty sure."

"Well, then it's probably for the best she resigned if the professional line is blurred."

I wanted to throw my glass at Nathan's head. His logical simplification of the situation irked me. He didn't get why I couldn't lose Skylar. But she was mine. A possessive spark ignited within my chest. I refused to let her go. I could fix this.

Skylar

"Stay strong today," Bria said, handing me a to go mug of coffee.

I rolled my swollen eyes. I'd tried to take down the swelling with ice. The last thing I wanted was for Ben to know I'd spent the whole weekend crying over him. Thankfully, Bria worked her magic with concealer and now you could hardly tell.

"I already quit, Bria. There's nothing to stay strong about."

A loud thud made us both jump as we turned to our kitchen wall.

"Shit, who starts throwing things at seven in the morning?" Bria asked.

"We need to move," we both said simultaneously.

We both walked out the door and down the steps. I turned to head to the office but Bria grabbed my arm, pulling me back.

"I'm serious. Stay strong. He's going to beg you to stay."

"No he isn't," I muttered. While I had hoped he might bombard me with apologetic text messages this weekend, maybe even show up to my place with flowers, nothing of the sort had happened. It was past time I let this fantasy of Ben go and realize he was nothing more than my boss. And a shitty one with no boundaries at that.

"Yes, he is," Bria insisted. "Trust me. That guy knows he needs you. You do everything for him. Just promise me you won't go back."

"I promise, Bria. I'm done after day fourteen."

She still looked unconvinced.

I breathed out a sigh. "Look, if I'm being pathetically honest, the truth is that the idea of leaving him hurt too much. But now the thought of staying—of being around him—it's unbearable. I can't stay."

She nodded. "Good. We're done with that asshole."

"Right," I confirmed before we separated.

The entire walk to work my stomach flipped with anxiety. What would seeing him after Friday night be like?

"Morning!" Ben greeted me cheerily from his office. He strode out and placed a large coffee on my desk.

"Um morning?" I couldn't meet his eyes. What was he doing here? Ben had only gotten in before me a handful of times in the entire time I'd worked here.

"Thought you could use an extra dose of caffeine

this morning," he said, nudging the cup closer to me. "Vanilla almond latte. Your favorite."

His hopeful voice had me on high alert. Was he sucking up to me?

I lifted my to go mug from home in his direction before sitting down. "Thanks, but I already have coffee."

"Oh." He sounded dejected as he picked the cup back up. He lingered as I powered on my computer. "How was the rest of your weekend?" he asked.

I shot a glare in his direction. "Better than Friday night," I muttered under my breath. I knew he still heard me though.

"Right, of course." He shifted his feet. "I'm sorry again about that, Sky—"

I lifted my hand. "Please stop. It's fine. I don't want to discuss it anymore."

To my genuine shock, Ben Mead kneeled down at my desk and placed his hands near mine. I had no choice but to look at him now that he was eye level.

"What are you doing?"

"It's not fine," he said, eyes pleading. "I was an asshole. I don't deserve you, Sky."

I lifted my eyebrows. *You can say that again.*

"Look, I won't hold a grudge against you, okay?" I said. "I've really enjoyed most of my time here the past three years. But I should have moved on a while ago. Now, if you'll excuse me, I really should get to work. I've got a lot to do before next week."

His face looked panicked. "So you won't reconsider? I need you—"

"I meant it, Ben. I'm sorry but my notice is in effect.

I'm drafting an e-mail to HR now. As for my replacement, I'll start looking for applicants this afternoon. I promise I'll find someone even better."

Ben hung his head and shook it. "That isn't possible."

The sadness in his face almost caused me to second guess my decision. But I knew his concern wasn't because he was losing me. It was because he was losing his spineless assistant that would drop everything to do whatever he asked.

He didn't care for me the same way I did for him, and it was past time I stepped out of my delusional fantasy world and faced the cold truth of reality.

Benjamin Mead would never love me back.

Ben

"Morning," I greeted Sky as she strode into the office. Ever since she'd given her notice, I'd started making a habit of beating her in every morning. I hoped that by making her life as easy as possible, she might change her mind and continue on as my assistant.

"Morning, Ben," she said coolly.

I flinched at her iciness. Well, it was hardly iciness, but she greeted me with none of the warmth and genuine excitement that she used to. I hated looking back and thinking about all those moments I took for granted.

"Any exciting plans this weekend?" I asked, trying to sound non-committal. Typically, I lived for the weekends. While my partner, Nathan, worked nonstop, I on the other hand appreciated letting loose. My weekends were usually reserved for endless dates with models and spending an exorbitant amount of money. My escapades typically made front page news much to Nathan's and the board's dismay.

"Mostly job hunting," she said. The words were like a knife to my heart.

"Sky, please." I let my defenses drop as I pleaded with her. "Rethink this. Did you even consider my offer?"

She sighed and turned away from her computer. "I already told you, it's not about the money."

I had taken Nathan's advice and offered her a raise. While I started at fifteen percent, that had quickly turned to offering to double it after she rejected each proposal. This week I kept telling myself I could change her mind. But as Friday came, and the last weekend before she left loomed ahead, I had migrated into full on panic mode.

"Sky, I already promised I'd never do anything like last week again. Please give me one more shot. I won't take you for granted again."

She sighed in frustration and rose from her chair. Grabbing my arm, she tugged me into my office and closed the door behind us.

"Why do you insist on torturing me like this?" she demanded, her typically sweet demeanor nowhere in sight.

"*I'm* torturing *you*? The idea of losing you is literally eating me alive. I've been a mess all week. You should have seen me at the board meeting on Wednesday. I completely tanked because all I could think about was this countdown you set in motion."

"*I* set it in motion?" She glared at me. "I think we both know there's more to the story than that."

I ran a hand over my face in exasperation. "So

because I don't have feelings for you you're punishing me like this? I'm sorry I can't be the guy you want me to be, but it seems hardly fair to leave me like this."

Her mouth hung open in shock before she snapped it closed and leveled me with a glare. She shook her head.

"Life's not fair," she muttered, averting her gaze from mine.

I saw the hurt in her eyes, and I wished I could take back my harsh words. We both knew she had a lot more valid reasons for quitting—probably more than I could count. And saying I didn't have feelings for her probably wasn't the whole truth. But regardless of what I felt, I couldn't be the kind of guy she needed. I was destined to a life of one-night stands and cheap hook ups. Nothing like what she deserved.

"I'm sorry, I didn't mean for it to come out that way," I said gently, tilting my head to try and catch her eye. She shifted to avoid me. I breathed out a frustrated sigh. "I'm just at my wit's end. I only have next week before you're supposedly leaving and I'm running out of ideas to keep you."

She finally looked up. I wished I could reach out and bridge the distance I had created between us. It was hard to remember a time when banter came easily between us. Not seeing her face every day would kill me.

"Did you think I'd stay here forever? I need to move on professionally."

"I can give you a promotion." I smacked my forehead. "Shit. Why didn't I think of that earlier. We could draw you up a new offer and title—"

My words cut off as she shook her head sadly. "It's about more than that. I can't work for you anymore. It's cruel of you to make this harder on me than it already is. You know how I feel—trust me I wish I hid it better, but it's useless now. I need to move on, and the only way I'm going to do that is by leaving."

Her words crushed me. *Move on.* That was the last thing I wanted her to do. I wanted to hold her tight and never let her out of my sight.

"I have to go look at resumes," she said, pushing past me. In a daze, I let her go. "I'm setting up interviews next week. I know you think I'm irreplaceable, but I promise we'll find someone just as good. You won't even notice I'm gone." She smiled sadly and moved out of the room as I fell back into my chair.

That's where she was wrong. Her absence would leave a gigantic hole in my life. She was anything but replaceable.

"WHAT ARE YOU STILL DOING HERE?" NATHAN ASKED, entering my line of sight and blocking my view of Skylar. I raised my eyes to look at him.

"It's only six," I said.

"Exactly. You always leave early on Fridays. Remember when I tried to set a company policy involving staying until at least five? You had the whole company up in anarchy."

"Because that was—and is—a ridiculous policy," I

muttered. "If you were the only boss around here, everyone would quit."

He raised his eyebrows. "Harsh criticism considering the only person that has quit lately was a direct result of your actions."

"Shut up," I snapped, glowering at him.

He smirked and took the seat opposite of me.

Before I could dig into him for being an asshole and rubbing something in my face that I already felt guilty enough about, Sky stood up from her desk and peeked her head in my door.

"Heading out now," she said. "I just sent you all the applicants for my replacement. Have a nice weekend."

I opened my mouth to say something, but she had already high tailed it out of there. My fist balled in frustration. I knew she saw Nathan's arrival as her perfect chance for escape. The past week, I'd cornered her every time she left the office to try and convince her to stay. Yesterday, I had even tried to follow her home like a stalker. I had stopped following her when I saw the defeated expression in her eyes. As much as I was hurting, I knew she was hurting ten times more.

"Find any good candidates?" Nathan asked after she'd gone.

"I haven't even looked," I said, rubbing my temple. "Fuck, Nathan. What am I going to do?"

He looked at me perplexed. "I don't understand why you're so upset. It's normal to have an employee move on. I know she's been an adequate assistant, but your visceral reaction makes no sense."

I groaned. This is what I got for trying to open up to Nathan. He only saw the world in black and white.

"This isn't about logic. I've grown attached—I care about Skylar. If she leaves, I won't see her again."

"And that's a problem," he said, as if trying to understand.

"Yes!" I exclaimed.

"I don't get it. You'll have a new assistant. It's not normal to be this upset about this."

"You're impossible," I muttered. "If you weren't so cold and emotionless, you'd get it."

His gaze hardened. "No, you're impossible. You won't admit to yourself that your feelings run deeper than that of a boss and his employee. I stand by what I said. It's *not* normal to be upset about this. Unless you're in love with her, that is."

My eyebrows shot up at his blunt words. "Bite your tongue. Benjamin Mead has never—and will never be in love."

What was the point? I'd seen all the good it had done for my parents. No, it was far better to remain unattached. No expectations meant no disappointment.

Nathan rolled his eyes, standing. "Whatever you say, but your actions don't match your words. If you don't do something about this soon it'll be too late and you'll regret it."

My mouth hung slack as he exited my office. Had Nathan really just given me relationship advice? Hell must have frozen over.

I tried to clear my head but thoughts of Sky ran through my mind. How was I supposed to make it the whole weekend without talking to her? Especially knowing just how limited our time together was?

Maybe if I showed her I could be a better guy she'd stay. If I didn't constantly throw my playboy ways in her face she could bear to be in the same room as me. But I understood her hesitance—why would she believe I changed after all I'd put her through? I would have to prove it to her, and I hardly had time to do it. Actions spoke louder than words, and I'd have to think of something fast if I had any hope of keeping her.

Skylar

"APPLICATION NUMBER FIFTEEN COMPLETED," I CHEERED.

Bria walked over from the kitchen and high fived me.

"Hell yeah," she said. "Companies are going to be fighting over you at this rate."

I sighed. "We'll see. So far I've only set up a few interviews."

Money was tight enough as it was, and I didn't want to stretch it any further by being unemployed for more than a week or two. Something needed to pan out quickly.

"You'll find something," Bria insisted. "You're the smartest person I know. You've honestly been wasting your potential working for he-who-shall-not-be-named all these years."

"Stop referring to him like that." I laughed, rolling my eyes.

"He doesn't deserve to be called by name after all those years taking advantage of you."

Dropping my gaze back to my computer, I tried to push thoughts of Ben away. This upcoming week would be our last together. Seeing him every day was a comfort —and despite my best efforts of trying to change, I was still in love with him. Part of me worried I always would be. I hated that I couldn't be like everyone else and chalk it up to a silly unrequited crush. He meant more to me than that.

Voices carried through our thin walls and Bria groaned loudly. "What the hell. Now they're fighting on a Sunday morning? Is nothing sacred?"

I closed my computer as Stella and Stanley continued to yell. No sense in trying to be productive when I couldn't hear myself think.

Bria held her ear up to the wall. "If I'm hearing correctly, she's upset because he went out with a female coworker last night."

I shook my head. "She could really do better."

Bria threw her hand back and banged against the wall. "You can do better!" She yelled.

A muffled, "Mind your own business!" carried over, and Bria and I cackled with laughter. Maybe it was dark to laugh at our constantly feuding neighbors, but if we didn't try to see the humor in our shitty living situation we might cry.

There was a knock at the door and Bria and I both looked at each other, frozen.

"Shit, is that them?" I asked.

Bria looked panicked but then shook her head. "No, it can't be. I still hear them yelling."

We both looked at the door and then back to each

other in confusion. No one ever knocked. Who would it be?

We both stood there in silence.

"Maybe they'll go away," I whispered.

Another urgent knock caused us both to jump.

Bria took an exaggerated deep breath in and then moved to the door. She checked the peephole before jerking away.

"It's some guy," she said.

"Some guy?" I repeated.

She looked again. This time when she pulled away, she looked angry. "What does Ben look like again?"

"What?" I gasped, leaping up from the couch.

Bria barricaded herself in front of the door. "Don't answer it," she demanded. "Where does he get off coming to your apartment?"

"Bria, I have to answer it. Come on." I tried to reach around her, but she blocked me.

"I can hear you," Ben's muffled voice came through the door.

"See," I said.

Bria let out a huff and then spun around, throwing open the door.

"Benjamin Mead," she said it like his name was a dirty word.

He raised his eyebrows and looked from her to me. He was dressed more casually than I had ever seen him in a gray hoodie, jeans, and tennis shoes. I was thankful I had changed out of my pajamas today and was at least wearing a cute pair of leggings and a cropped sweatshirt.

"Hi," he said, attempting to charm Bria with a smile. "You seem to know me, but I don't have the pleasure."

She glared at him. "I'm Skylar's best friend, Bria. Although maybe you'd know that if you ever bothered to ask her personal information. You're too busy treating her like a servant."

"Bria!" I exclaimed.

Ben's eyebrows shot up. "No, that's fair." He looked over her head to meet my eyes. "I should have treated her better."

I couldn't help it, I smiled at his sincerity. Damnit. My will was weak.

"Whatever," Bria grumbled. "I was about to head out to study. You going to be alright?" she asked, glancing back at me.

"I'm fine."

Bria pushed past Ben. "Don't try anything funny."

"Got it." He saluted her as she walked away.

He stood there awkwardly in the doorframe.

"Oh, come in," I said.

He stepped inside and he looked so out of place in my shoebox of an apartment. I felt self-conscious of my space—especially knowing the mansion he called home.

"This is where you live?" Ben asked, observing everything.

"Yep," I said just as Stanley and Stella started up yelling again. It sounded like a pan had been thrown.

"What the fuck?" Ben looked at the wall. "What's going on over there?"

I rolled my eyes. "It's our neighbors. They're always fighting."

His eyebrows knit. "They always yell like that?"

"Always," I said.

As if on cue, more sounds of loud clattering came from next door. Ben looked to the wall and then back to me.

"Is it... Is it safe here?" he asked.

The hair on the back of my neck bristled.

"Just because I don't live in some fancy townhouse doesn't mean it's unsafe."

"Shit, Sky. I didn't mean it like that." He ran his fingers through his hair. "I just hate that you have to listen to that every day."

I sighed, turning away from him. "I'm used to it."

He didn't look convinced. "You know, the door to this building doesn't even lock. I just walked right in."

"It's convenient not having to carry another key around."

He groaned as if my admittance tortured him. "I really hate that."

"Look, it's a safe area," I said in frustration.

"You promise?" Ben looked at me expectantly.

"Well, safe-ish." I lifted my hand and teetered it back and forth. This area was fine, but I couldn't deny that I wouldn't walk around alone at night. Plus, there may or may not have been a break-in on this block last week. I wasn't admitting that to Ben, though.

"Sky." He said my name like he was disciplining a toddler.

I threw my arms in the air in exasperation. "What do you want from me? It's cheap and I can walk to work."

"I need to be paying you a hell of a lot more then," he muttered His eyes bore into mine, and I forced myself to stare back.

"Won't matter after next week."

Hurt crossed his face but he hid it well. "Then I'm going to give you a sizable bonus," he insisted, looking around my apartment.

My defenses raised. "That's not necessary."

He blew out a breath. "Do you at least carry pepper spray? A Taser?"

"Ben," I said in a clipped tone. "Did you come here for a reason? Or is criticizing my apartment the only thing on your agenda?"

"No—I mean sorry. I came over because I need your help with something."

My eyebrow shot up and my guard went on high alert. Could this be another scandal cover up?

"On a Sunday?" I asked warily.

His eyes widened as he took in my expression. "Nothing like what you're thinking."

"I don't know. Do you really need me? I'm applying for jobs."

He clutched his chest and smiled sheepishly at me. "Ouch. There's a knife right to the heart."

"Ben, be serious for a minute."

"I am. Do you need me to write a letter of recommendation? I promise I'll sing your praises. Although maybe if I tell everyone you stole from me or something, you won't get hired and you'll be forced to stay with me—"

"Ben!"

He held his hands up, chuckling. "I'm kidding. I'd never do that."

"What do you need, then?" I repeated the question.

"Come with me and find out." He jerked his head to my front door. "I promise it won't take all day and it'll be a hell of a lot better than listening to your neighbors yelling."

"AN ANIMAL SHELTER?" I LOOKED FROM THE INDUSTRIAL building back at Ben.

Our car ride here had been awkward as he tried to make small talk. He offered to stop at every food place we passed in case I wanted something. I almost felt bad for him. He was trying so hard to connect with me. But then I remembered everything he had asked me to do over the years, and my sympathy quickly dissipated.

"Yep," he said, stuffing his hands into his hoodie pocket.

I could tell he was nervous. In my three years working for him, I'd hardly ever seen Ben nervous. He was just one of those people, always charming and collected no matter what was going on with the company or his personal life.

"What are we doing here?" I asked, my voice sounding utterly defeated.

"Come inside and I'll tell you." He nodded toward the entrance as his eyes searched mine.

I dropped my gaze to my feet and trudged ahead. Didn't he realize that spending the day with him was slowly killing me inside? Seeing him so casual outside of work and taking every opportunity to be nice to me was just making this harder. I hated the way sitting in his car could almost make it feel like we were together. He didn't even realize how severely he affected me—either that or he didn't care. I hoped it was the former. Because it hurt to think about him manipulating me like this to spend the day with him, knowing how hard it was for me. I would rather think of him as clueless, to be honest.

Walking through the front door, we were immediately greeted by a volunteer in a blue vest.

"Happy Sunday!" She smiled cheerily. "What brings you in today?"

"I'd like to adopt a dog," Ben said confidently.

My mouth hung open. "Excuse me?"

He smiled down at me. "You heard right."

"But you don't do commitment or responsibility," I pointed out.

"Hey, I'm responsible."

I arched a brow, thinking of all the times I'd cleaned up one of his many messes.

He pinched the bridge of his nose as if reading my thoughts. "Okay, well, I'm responsible about some things."

"If you say so," I said as we followed the volunteer over to a computer.

"Just fill out the information here. Once you're done,

I'll take you back to look at the dogs to see if you can find a match."

"Perfect. Thanks." Ben sat at the computer and squinted at the screen.

I hovered behind him, still uncertain why he brought me here.

"And you're wrong by the way," Ben said.

"Huh?"

"I'm going to start doing commitment starting today. I need some stability in my life."

I sighed as if reasoning with a child. "A dog is a lot of work."

He nodded, still filling out the forms. "I know, which is why I spent all day yesterday researching. I already bought food, a crate, and toys. I even had a doggy door installed. Plus I found a dog walker to let them out when I have to spend long days at the office."

I sat down, regarding him. "Wow, you really have put a lot of thought into this." He looked over at me earnestly. "I know I can be an immature, dense jerk. But I don't want to be this guy forever."

"That's good," I said, searching his face. "I still don't get why I'm here though."

His eyes darted across my face before he moved them back to his screen. "Because you're the only one worth proving myself to," he muttered.

My breath caught in my throat as I sat there not knowing what to say. How could this be the same guy that called me a week ago to kick out his one-night stand? Was he really changing?

Stop that right now, the logical part of my brain finally chimed in.

I looked to my hands and picked a cuticle while Ben finished up. This was all a ploy—get me to see he's changing so that maybe I'll stay. With my weak resolve, it wasn't a bad plan. But little did he know, my heart had been mauled one too many times to fall for this.

Ben

DAY 9: SUNDAY

A BLACK LAB MIX JUMPED INTO MY ARMS AS I CROUCHED on the mat in the small room used for meet-and-greets. I laughed as I fell backward and rubbed the dog's head. He moved on to Skylar who sat cross-legged on the mat. He pushed his head against her arm, begging for a pet. She laughed before taking both hands and scratching his ears.

"He likes you," I said, grinning. "He's got good taste."

She rolled her eyes. I longed for the days when she looked at me like I was something special. It killed me how much I took those days for granted.

"I like him too." She got eye level with him before he licked her. "I mean look at this face."

Buddy, the dog, moved away from her and to my lap. He had immediately taken a liking to me after we walked the aisles of dogs available for adoption. It broke my heart to see them all in there. It broke my heart even more when Sky said something about wishing she could adopt but not being able to afford to.

What the hell kind of salary was I paying her? I wanted to kick my own ass for allowing her to stay in an apartment in a bad area of town. How could I have been so fucking clueless? I needed to speak with payroll immediately. Even if I couldn't convince her to stay—which for my own sanity I told myself I'd be able to do—she would be getting a sizeable exit bonus. To hell with policy, I hated myself for underpaying her all these years and never even realizing it. What kind of ass was I?

"You want to come home with me, Buddy?" I asked looking into the dogs deep brown eyes.

He licked my face and I laughed. "I think he's the one," I said, looking at Sky.

The volunteer stuck her head back in. "Did you two find a match?"

"I think so." I couldn't keep the grin off my face.

"Awh, he loves you two. I can tell. Is this your first dog as a couple?" she asked. "That's a big step."

My heart sank as I watched Skylar's face go from happiness to dread. "He's my boss," she muttered.

"And friend," I added, narrowing my eyes.

Maybe I couldn't be what she wanted me to be, but to say our relationship was purely professional made me irrationally angry. I cared about Sky more than most people—hell maybe even anyone. I meant it when I said she was the only person worth proving myself to.

How had I gotten myself in such a messy predicament?

"Well, Buddy here seems like he would be more than happy to go home with you today," the volunteer continued, sensing the tension rolling off of Sky and me. "He is due for some shots, though. You can wait around, but it will be a few hours."

I glanced at Sky. "We'll go get a bite to eat and then I'll come back?" It came out like a question. I knew she was likely eager to get away from me, but I wasn't ready to let her out of my sight yet.

Spending this time with her—outside of work—felt deliciously normal, and I didn't want it to end. Plus, she had even graced me with a few smiles. An expression I'd hardly seen from her this past week.

"Perfect," the girl said, taking Buddy from me and exiting the room. "I have your number. I can text you when he's ready to be picked up."

"See you soon, Buddy," I said giving his head one final pet.

Skylar stood and brushed off her pants. She eyed me cautiously. I wished I could have back that lighthearted moment we were sharing just minutes ago.

"I should probably get home," she said. "Don't worry about driving me. I can take a cab."

I reached for her arm and squeezed it lightly. "Please let me buy you lunch."

She searched my eyes and I hated how much hurt I saw there. She finally sighed and I knew I'd won. Although seeing how much the thought of spending the next few hours with me pained her, I wasn't sure it could actually be construed as a win.

Once back in the car, I drove us in silence to a

nearby diner. My brain screamed at me to say something. Fight for her.

But I kept coming up blank. Nathan's words kept ringing in my ears.

She's just your assistant.

While my gut reaction was to oppose that simplistic thought, he was right. I hadn't claimed Sky in any way. She wasn't mine. I had made it clear to her that nothing would happen between us. But she had made it clear that she couldn't offer me only her friendship. I looked over to see her mouthing the words to the song. Her blond hair tangled around one of her fingers.

I wasn't sure I could offer her just friendship either.

I pulled into the parking lot and exited the car. I moved around to get Skylar's door, but she was already on the ground closing it behind her. Her eyes widened when she looked up to see me hovering next to her door.

I scratched the back of my neck. "I was going to get that for you."

"The door?" she looked at me like I had lost my mind.

I suppose I probably had. Nothing about my behavior this past week was rational.

We walked into the diner and took a seat at a booth in the back. She ordered waffles even though it was past noon.

"What?" she asked, putting the menu away and assessing my smirk.

"Who gets waffles for lunch?" I asked, teasing her.

"Hey, it's *brunch* not lunch."

I tilted my head. "I guess that's fair."

She sat there, avoiding my eye contact and shifting in her seat while I fought desperately to think of something brilliant to say.

I sighed, rubbing my face. "I miss how things used to be with us," I admitted.

She looked up, her eyes softening for a moment before she looked down at the table. "I don't know what you want me to say, Ben."

I clenched my hand into a fist, looking for some way to release this energy.

"Look, I know I've been acting distant ever since...you know." I didn't want to mention our kiss again knowing how much it affected her—hell, affected me. "I was a jerk to have you clean up my last scandal after our...moment. But I was just so used to relying on you for everything. I fucked up and I know it. I understand why you decided to leave, but you have to know how sorry I am." My eyes silently pleaded with her to look up at me.

She glanced up at me and I felt relief to see none of the recent animosity there. She took a shaky breath. "It's okay. I'm not angry at you."

"Then why won't you talk to me?" I asked.

"Because talking to you is harder than it used to be," she whispered.

I wanted to reach for her, pull her to me, but I knew I couldn't. I tilted my head down instead, keeping my eyes trained on her.

"It doesn't have to be. I'm still me. The same guy that talked you through your first big presentation. The same guy that you cried to that one late night because you missed your family. And you're still the girl I can open up to more than anyone." I thought about all of the dirty details I revealed to her about my cold family throughout the years. She hadn't pitied me for any of them. Instead, she always gave a sympathetic ear and made me feel like someone cared.

She looked at me, her eyes glassy. "And that's the problem."

My jaw clenched. Shit. This was harder than I thought it'd be. What kind of selfish jerk was I? Trying to convince her to stay when being around me was clearly causing her pain.

But I cared about her. No matter how complicated the situation was, I couldn't deny that.

The waitress came back and set down our plates. Skylar picked up her fork and started to eat, likely grateful for the distraction.

"I don't know what I'm going to do without you," I said.

She frowned. "We have a bunch of interviews next week. I promise someone will be just as good."

That's not what I meant. If I was being honest with myself, work was the last thing I was thinking about when I thought about her absence.

As we sat there in continued silence, frustration bloomed in my chest.

Fuck. Why couldn't I just be honest with her and myself about what I was really feeling? Nathan was right. This wasn't normal. I didn't act this way around everyone. She was the most important person in my life

—work aside. But admitting that could change everything.

We finished eating and I paid the bill. A knot formed in my chest as I knew my time with her today was concluding and I hadn't made any progress on improving our situation. She was still leaving next week and I would have no reason to see her ever again.

The drive back to her apartment was quiet and somber. A thousand thoughts weighed on my mind.

"Well, this is me," she said as I pulled up to her place.

"Unfortunately," I muttered.

She narrowed her eyes. "I could use without the offhand comments about my apartment, thank you very much."

She moved to grab the door handle but I instinctively grabbed her arm. "Sky, you know I care about you, right? As more than an assistant?"

Her eyebrows shot up in surprise.

"I've never really told you that before and I should have. You've always been more than that to me. I want you to know that."

She opened her mouth, her eyes full of shock and...something else I couldn't identify. Before she could say anything, a loud knock sounded against her window.

I turned and saw her obnoxious roommate with a scowl on her face.

"Welcome back," Bria said, glaring at me.

I supposed I deserved most of the hate she had wielded in my direction today.

Sky tore her gaze from me. "I better get going," she

said. "Thanks for lunch. And I'm happy you're getting a dog. I think it'll be really good for you."

She smiled at me and my heart tugged at the simple gesture.

"I'll see you tomorrow," I said, wishing for nothing more than to be able to pull her toward me.

As she walked away, pain surged through me.

Why couldn't I just admit to her everything that I was feeling?

Skylar

"I HAVE TWO YEARS OF EXPERIENCE AS AN EXECUTIVE assistant to the CEO at my last company." The blonde bombshell continued to list off her accolades as I nodded in approval. She was stunning—and more than qualified. I tried to ignore the pang of jealousy at the thought of this woman becoming Ben's new assistant and working closely with him every day.

I'm sure he'd have no issue crossing the professional line with her, I thought bitterly.

When I glanced at Ben to gauge his reaction to her, I found him studying me instead. His intensity sent a chill down my spine.

"We'll be in touch," Ben said abruptly, standing from his desk.

I stood, shaking my head with confusion. This was our third interview of the day and I had led them all. Ben had barely acknowledged the candidates and hadn't asked any meaningful questions all day.

The candidate walked out of the room with a

lingering look back at Ben. He didn't even give her a cursory glance.

"Was she not a good fit?" I asked, raising an eyebrow. I would have thought her long legs and pouty lips would have caused Ben to offer her the job right on the spot.

He shrugged. "I don't think she's right for this."

"Why?" I pressed.

He crossed his arms. "Do you really want to know?"

"Of course."

He leaned closer. "Because she isn't you."

I rolled my eyes. "Ben, I'm leaving Friday whether you like it or not. Ignoring perfectly qualified candidates isn't going to change that. It's just going to leave you high and dry with no assistant."

He searched my eyes before letting out a frustrated sigh and leaning back in his chair. "I know that."

"Then what are you playing at?"

He ran a hand through his hair, clearly agitated. "I don't even know anymore. You tell me."

I shook my head. This man infuriated me. He had been acting like me putting in my notice had completely upturned his entire life. He was making every step of this challenging. He didn't seem to care that I couldn't be around him. It hurt my heart far too much. No, instead he was entirely preoccupied with what my absence would do to him, not what his presence did to me.

"I don't know what you want me to say," I responded, standing and gathering my things. "You've been acting weird about this and it's time you accept it."

"I can't accept it," he snapped.

I whipped my head around, surprised by his panicked tone. He gripped the edge of his desk, his knuckles turning white.

"What is going on with you?" I asked, genuinely concerned. Ben had never seemed the type to abhor change so vehemently. Sure, I thought he might be upset when I gave my notice but I had never expected such an extreme reaction.

He stood up, his expression softening. "Look, I think we should talk about us—"

A knock at the door signaled Nathan arriving for Ben's next meeting.

He walked in and nodded at me as I shot one last sympathetic look toward Ben.

"I promise, any of those candidates will do a great job. You don't need to worry so much," I reassured him.

He blew out a breath and hung his head before shaking it in defeat.

Nathan arched a brow and gave me a confused look. I just shrugged before leaving the room.

I settled into my desk and tried to ignore the forlorn look on Ben's face. What the hell was going on with him? He was acting like my leaving was the end of the world. I didn't want to entertain the small hope that maybe his feelings ran deeper than friendship but I couldn't shake the thought. Bria would murder me if she knew I was having this fantasy again.

My imagination ran wild as I thought back to all the reasons my feelings for him grew in the first place. How he always asked how I was doing. How anytime we had to stay late we'd order takeout and have a running competition for which place had the best crab wontons. Hell, he even asked me to pick him up from his wisdom teeth removal appointment. He was so drugged up when I brought him up his front steps, he told me I was his favorite person in the world.

My cheeks burned at the memories. No, I was not crazy. Maybe he would always refuse to admit it, but Benjamin Mead harbored some sort of feelings for me. Maybe it wasn't love, but it was…something.

I groaned and placed my head in my hands. This exact line of thinking was precisely the reason I needed to get the hell out of here. If my parents knew I was wasting away as someone's assistant and putting my career and dating life on hold, they'd be horrified and force me on the first flight back home.

Sighing, I reached back out to the woman that just left and asked if she'd be open to another phone interview. Whether Ben wanted to face the truth or not, I was leaving. I only had to survive a few more days in his presence without losing it.

Ben

"Was that woman I saw walking out of here earlier your new assistant?" Nathan asked, crossing his legs at the head of the conference room.

"No," I huffed, still irritated Skylar's resolve to quit remained strong. It was probably cocky of me to think I could change her mind. Deep down, I knew I was trying to take advantage of her feelings for me to get her to stay.

What the hell was wrong with me?

Nathan raised his eyebrows in surprise. "She seemed just like your type. I thought for sure you'd jump at the chance to have her working under you."

He was right—she was my typical type. But the thought of flirting with her held absolutely zero appeal. What had gotten into me?

Skylar had gotten into me.

"What's wrong with me, Nathan? I'm not myself?"

Nathan arched an eyebrow, likely surprised I chose to open up to him at all. We'd known each other for years after becoming college roommates and starting this company together. But we were so incredibly different, our relationship never really evolved past partners. While I was the philandering playboy, he was the cold, logical workaholic.

"If by 'not myself' you mean you've stopped dragging your name through the mud in the tabloids every other day, than I'm in no rush for your true self to return."

I ignored him. "You're right about that woman that interviewed. She was stunning. Yet I barely even registered her. Why is that?"

He looked at me blankly. "You seriously think I hold the answer?" Nathan had never had a relationship in his entire life. Except his reasons were because he saw no appeal in them. Unlike me, whose parents absolutely wrecked the construct of love and marriage and made it seem like a fantasy instead of something real.

"Something is wrong with me and I can't snap out of it," I said.

"Maybe it will be better once Skylar leaves."

I scowled. "*Nothing* will be better when she leaves."

Nathan sighed and evaluated me. "You love her," he stated simply.

My jaw dropped at his allegation. "I definitely do not love her. Care for her? Maybe. But love her? No fucking way."

He shook his head. "Love is illogical, and you're being the definition of illogical. It's the only reason I can think of that explains why you've been so off these past two weeks."

My jaw went slack.

There was no way I was in love with Skylar. Sure, maybe I cared about her. Of course, I couldn't imagine my life without her. Yes, she made every second of everyday better. But in love with her?

No way.

Although to be fair, was I even sure what love felt like? It's not like I had experienced it growing up. My family treated each other like we were in competition and the prize was a trust fund.

"I am not in love with her," I deflected, but my words weren't as sure as I wanted them to be.

Nathan stood up, brushing his hands on his pants. "I have no interest in this conversation anymore."

"Wait!" I called.

He paused.

"How-how can you be sure?"

He looked back at me. "I'm not," he said simply. "I likely know even less about love than you do. But there's a reason you're fighting this so hard, and it's definitely not because you can't find someone to replace her as your assistant."

As soon as he left the room, I collapsed against the chair, burying my head in my hands.

I wasn't in love with Skylar.

Right?

Skylar

THE OFFICE HADN'T COME TO LIFE YET THAT MORNING. Taking in my surroundings, it felt surreal that I'd only have a few more days in this setting. I still remembered my first day here and how out of place I'd felt. I hadn't known the right thing to wear or how to behave, and I was so nervous to meet Ben. I had been hired by a temp agency and I was scared to meet this playboy millionaire that was notorious in the tabloids. But Ben wasn't at all what I imagined. He greeted me warmly and was kind when I asked questions.

Nathan actually made me cry that first day because I had messed up a simple email forward—now I realized that wasn't personal, he's just cold like that. Ben had found me trying to hide my tears by the coffee maker and took me out to lunch. He'd given me a pep talk and told me I belonged there just like everyone else. Our relationship only grew from there.

Tears burned at the back of my eyes as I thought about all we'd been through. How sad was it that the most significant relationship in my life was my boss? Shaking my head, I drove away the thoughts. All I could do was focus on the positives. Ben would move on, and I'd move on. I would get a life of my own and stop getting caught up on the fantasy of us.

"Hey, Skylar." Ben greeted me with a smile as he walked over and set a fresh latte on my desk.

"Morning." I smiled genuinely at him. Knowing I likely wouldn't see him again after Friday had me unable to give the cold shoulder any longer. Instead I wanted to drink up every friendly gesture, every wink, every smile.

He sat down on the edge of my desk, crossing his arms. "Do you have plans after work?"

"Just more job hunting," I admitted.

He winced but didn't drop his smile.

"I really need your help with something."

"Adopting another dog?"

He chuckled. "I think Buddy is going to be an only child. He's a handful."

"I told you it was a big responsibility."

He shrugged, staring at me. "It's worth it."

"What did you need my help with then?"

"YOU REALLY COULDN'T MANAGE THIS BY YOURSELF?" I asked as Ben came out in a different impeccably designed suit.

"I trust your taste," he said, turning from me and looking at the floor length mirror.

"Champagne?" The sales associate offered me a glass.

"Why not?" I muttered, taking it from her. I wasn't sure why Ben had insisted I go suit shopping with him tonight. I knew there was a big benefit gala that he and Nathan had to attend tomorrow, but I'm sure the man had plenty of perfectly suitable options for such an occasion.

It seemed like he was looking for any excuse to spend time with me.

I took a sip of the champagne and enjoyed the fizzy bubbles bursting on my tongue.

Ben turned and looked at himself in the mirror, a smirk gracing his face.

"Do I look okay?" he asked.

I rolled my eyes. "You always look okay and you know it."

He grinned, eyeing me from the mirror. "But I love it when you say it."

My cheeks flushed at the comment.

"So did you call back any of the assistant candidates?" I asked, changing the subject.

He didn't answer me right away, looking off to the side.

"Ben," I chastised.

He looked down, rubbing his neck. "I haven't had a chance."

"It only takes a few minutes," I said. Why was he making this impossible? I guess it wasn't my responsibility if he chose to be without an assistant after my absence.

He shrugged, not making eye contact. "Maybe I'm still hoping there's a shot you'll change your mind."

"Not happening."

I frowned as pain tugged at my heart. Why was he doing this to me? Every day he looked at me with these puppy dog eyes like I was ruining his life. Why couldn't he just let me go?

Ben stepped off the platform and took a seat on the bench next to me. "What's going through your mind? Your face just fell."

His eyes roamed over mine, looking for an answer.

"Just tired," I said.

He shook his head. "That's bullshit."

I sighed. "This is hard for me, okay? I don't know what you want me to say. You think I'm excited not to see you every day? Newsflash I'm not."

I felt vulnerable and raw under his gaze. Why did he always have all the power?

He frowned. "Then stay."

"I can't."

"Why not?"

"Because it's too hard." My eyes moved to the floor.

He grabbed my hands and the shock of his touch caused me to jerk my head up. His eyes pleaded with mine. "This is killing me, Sky."

I opened and closed my mouth. "Why are you doing this?" I whispered. "Please stop toying with me."

"I'm not," he protested, running his hand through his hair. "Sky, I—"

"Is that the one." The sales associate returned and gestured to Ben's suit.

"This will be fine." he mumbled, not taking his eyes —or hands—off me. "We'll be needing a dress too— formal," he added.

My eyes narrowed. Was he really ordering a dress for a date in front of me?

"I have to go," I said, rising.

Ben stood hurriedly. "Not until you try on a few dresses."

"What?"

He looked at me determinedly. "You're coming with me tomorrow night."

Ben

I pulled the car up to Skylar's shabby apartment building and sighed in defeat. The fact that she lived here frustrated the hell out of me. As I approached the front door, the yelling carried out to the street. God, her neighbors were at it again.

I wished I could just scoop her up and—

And what? Take her home?

Fuck, my thoughts were a mess. Making her come to this benefit with me tonight was probably a mistake. Just a misguided attempt to be close to her for one more evening.

I knocked on her door while having half a mind to just walk away and tell her I didn't need her to come tonight after all.

Why couldn't I just let her go?

Then the door opened and it felt like the wind got knocked out of me.

Skylar stood there in the black gown she had picked out yesterday. It hugged her waist and flowed down the rest of her body perfectly. Her soft blonde hair was pinned up by the nape of her neck. Her wide eyes assessed me and I hated how unnerved she always looked around me lately. I sucked in a breath, finally remembering to breathe.

"You look beautiful," I murmured, my eyes completely fixed on her.

"Ahem," Bria cleared her throat as she stood behind Sky, arms crossed. "No funny business tonight."

"Bria," Skylar groaned.

I saluted her roommate and put on my best charming smile. "I promise to get her home in one piece." Although her dress was giving me different thoughts.

"Her curfew is midnight," Bria added.

"One," I countered.

Skylar sighed. "I'm not a teenager going to prom you know."

"Shoot, I forgot your corsage," I teased.

She shook her head, biting back a smile. "Let's go."

"THIS IS HELL," NATHAN MUTTERED. HOURS OF mingling would exhaust even the most charismatic of people. For someone like Nathan, it would likely take him at least a week to recover from the socializing he'd need to do at this benefit.

"You're fine," I insisted, not taking my eyes off Sky. She was still talking to the wife of one of our board members. She had spent all evening charming everyone she met. I felt proud to have her on my arm. For at least one night, I could pretend she was mine. I didn't want to delve into why I wanted to feel that so badly.

"I can't believe you brought her here." Nathan tipped back his drink.

"She's good for my image," I said, not even trying to be defensive.

"It's inappropriate to bring your assistant as your date."

I didn't even bother correcting his usage of the word date.

"She won't be my assistant for long," I said, not keeping the bitterness out of my voice.

Nathan shook his head. "You're an idiot."

I scowled at him in response. "Excuse me."

"You could have her if you wanted to. Any moron can see that. And you clearly want her, but you're making yourself miserable. So what the hell are you doing?"

Narrowing my eyes, I swirled my drink.

"There's no future for us," I said. "I'm not the guy for her—fuck I'm not the guy for anyone."

Nathan shrugged. "I suppose I can relate to that. But if that's the narrative you're sticking with, stop moping around like your world is crumbling. Suck it up, say your goodbyes, and get back to being focused on work. A lot is going on with the talks of this merger."

He was right. I knew he was. Yet, saying goodbye still seemed unfathomable to me. Skylar glanced up and smiled at me and it felt like the whole party stopped. She looked at me like I was something special. I craved how she made me feel. She walked over to me and it felt like we were the only two people in the room. I would never get sick of this feeling.

"This is kind of fun," she said when she got to the table where Nathan and I stood at.

He scowled down at her. "What kind of sick joke is that?" he asked.

"I'm sorry." Her brow knit in confusion.

"I'm getting another drink," he mumbled before stalking off.

"What was that about?" she asked.

I carelessly rested my hand on hers. My heart swelled when she didn't pull away. "Don't mind Nathan. He's bitter about all the small talk and networking he's had to do tonight."

She sighed. "I think it's nice. It feels like I'm Cinderella at a ball or something."

I laughed. "I hope you won't make me track you down with a shoe at the end of the night."

"Well, the coach turning into a pumpkin checks out. This definitely isn't where I fit in."

"You fit in beautifully," I said.

Her eyes widened as I stared down at her.

"Benjamin, fancy seeing you here." I jerked my gaze toward the familiar voice.

My father of all people lingered next to our table. It wasn't my mother standing next to him, but a curvy brunette at least half his age. Although he didn't touch her, I'm sure they were sleeping together.

"Hi, Dad," I said, not bothering to mask the bitterness in my tone. "Where's mom tonight?"

He glared at me. "Your mother had a different event to attend. We can't be expected to be together all the time."

I wanted to laugh. They were never together.

"Right, of course. And who is this?" I lifted my glass at the woman to his left. "An intern perhaps? So good of you to take the youthful minds of America under your wing."

The woman giggled, oblivious to the jab at my father.

His mouth formed a tight, thin line. "This is Cynthia." He didn't elaborate much beyond that, which meant my guess of intern probably wasn't too far off. Jesus, he disgusted me.

"Classy," I murmured, glancing around the room. The last thing I wanted to do was be stuck in this conversation a moment longer.

"This is your secretary, right?" my father leered.

Rage bubbled to the surface at his condescending tone.

Before I could say anything, Skylar squeezed my arm—a gesture of reassurance that caused my heart to swell.

"It's Skylar. And I'm his assistant," she said, her tone one of fake politeness I had come to recognize over the years.

My dad ignored her, all his attention still focused on me.

"Bringing your assistant to a gala." He snorted, shaking his head. "Not so different from your old man after all," he added in a low voice.

His insinuation filled me with disgust. Me being here with Skylar wasn't anything like him being here with this woman. Skylar actually meant something to me—not that my father could understand what that must feel like. He was a heartless bastard.

I glanced down at Skylar's face to see anger etched there too. Good, I hoped she realized everything that came out of his mouth was complete and utter bullshit.

"Why don't you move along?" I asked. "Or do you have nothing better to do tonight than taunt me?"

He rolled his eyes and the woman he was with shifted uncomfortably next to him. "Don't be so dramatic, Benjamin. I have every right to stand here and talk to you, despite what you may think." He eyed me up and down with a look of disdain. "What is my prodigal son doing here anyway? I know my assistant forwards the family these big events, but you never usually show."

My grip tightened on my glass. God, he really could get under my skin like no one else.

"I'm here for Pulse. Our board members insisted we attend."

He looked bored. "I always forget about your silly little app."

Skylar squeezed my arm again and cleared her throat. "Excuse me sir, but doesn't it get exhausting?"

He arched an eyebrow and looked down at her for the first time. "Excuse me?"

She smiled sweetly. "Doesn't it get exhausting pretending you're unaware of how successful your son is? His company is all over any major tech publication.

Their IPO is heavily anticipated. Surely a big business mogul such as yourself would be aware of that."

My father's face turned beet red and my eyes grew wide as I stared down at Skylar with adoration. Her standing up for me had my chest puffing with pride. I loved having her by my side.

"I think I actually will go mingle," my father grumbled, pulling the young woman away with him like she was a dog instead of a person.

I turned back to Skylar. "That was amazing. You got rid of my father in record time."

"He's an asshole." Her eyes narrowed. "I hope you never doubt your worth or success because of him."

My mouth went dry at her sincere statement. I couldn't take it anymore. Grabbing her hand, I pulled her toward the side exit door.

"Where are we going?" she asked, but let me pull her along.

As soon as we were outside, away from the crowd, I spun her to face me. Before I could think twice about it, I cradled her soft cheeks in my hands and scanned her eyes. I slowly leaned in, worried she might back away. But she didn't. Instead, she bit her bottom lip in anticipation. I couldn't contain myself anymore. Dipping down, I met her waiting lips. They were soft and she tasted just like I remembered. My mouth moved carefully over hers as my hand dropped to her throat, gently tethering her to me. She felt too good to touch— dangerous even. She was the type of woman I could get lost in, the type of woman I could never tire of.

A soft sound came from her lips as they parted, and I

took the opportunity to slip my tongue inside. I flicked it against hers, enjoying the way she practically melted beneath my touch. My want for her became apparent quickly as my kiss grew hungrier. She kissed me back passionately, her hands moving to tangle themselves in my hair.

Breaking away, I searched her lust filled eyes before pressing my forehead against hers.

"I can't lose you," I muttered.

Skylar

IF ONLY BRIA COULD SEE MY DELUSIONAL SELF NOW—
seated on Ben's couch while he poured me a drink. She
would barge in here and drag me out before I could so
much as utter a single objection.

But he'd said he couldn't lose me.

While it wasn't exactly a declaration of love, it was
pretty close right? He had forced me to come to that
party and all night he couldn't take his eyes off me.
And then he did the unthinkable. He kissed me.
Maybe he had tried to hide from his feelings before,
but this felt different. It felt like he was finally ready to
open up to me. Maybe all my fantasies about us finally
ending up together weren't so pathetic and crazy
after all.

"Here you go," Ben said, handing me a glass of
something clear before sitting next to me on the couch.

"Thanks," I said shyly. Me ending up back at his
house was definitely a step further than the last time we
kissed at a party, and my nerves were getting the best of

me. I had thought about this moment for so long, I wasn't quite sure how to act now that it was finally here.

Ben looked at his lap and then back at me before taking a long sip of his drink. "I can't believe you're here," he admitted.

I let out a soft laugh, grateful he seemed just as perplexed by the situation as I was. "Me too."

He knocked back the rest of his drink and ran his hand through his hair. "When you gave me your notice two weeks ago, it sent me into this spiral of panic. It made me realize you're a hell of a lot more than my assistant."

I gulped as he gazed at me intensely before scooping up my hands in his.

"I didn't know what we had Sky—how special it was —until I almost lost it. You're the only person I'm excited to tell good news to. You're the only face I look forward to seeing every day. You're so kind and generous and smart." He shook his head, a small laugh escaping. "These past few days, I've been imagining life without you. As your final day loomed closer, I realized I couldn't even fathom it. I need you. I really do. Sky, please, please don't leave me."

His begging tone had butterflies exploding in my stomach.

"I don't want to lose you either," I admitted. "You must know how I feel for you after all this time. I think you're amazing, Ben. There's more to you than anyone gives you credit for."

Before I could lose my nerve, I set my drink down on the coffee table in front of the couch.

The look in his eyes when I took his glass and placed it on the table too made my breath catch. They were dark and full of need. It had been so long since someone had looked at me with hunger, I almost forgot what it felt like. Actually, come to think of it I'm not sure I'd ever been looked at the way Ben's eyes were consuming me right now.

"Sky, what are you doing?" he asked. His voice was low and thick with arousal.

I licked my lips, his eyes tracking the movement. Before I could think any more about it, I leaned forward and brushed my lips against his, ready to pick up where we had left off at the gala.

Ben's response was immediate and powerful. He growled low in his throat and wrapped his arms around me, hauling me against him. My lips parted in a gasp and he took advantage, his tongue tangling with mine.

Our mouths clashed in a heated kiss, teeth nipping, tongues exploring, lips caressing. It was as though a fire was set ablaze, and there was no hope of putting it out. I needed to get closer to him. I lifted my leg and placed it on Ben's other side, straddling his lap. His mouth tore away from mine for a minute as he searched my face.

"We shouldn't." He forced the words out as if they were painful. Now that I sat in his lap, I could feel just how badly his body wanted mine.

"I've been thinking about this for a long time, Ben," I whispered.

His body shuddered beneath mine at the sound of his name.

"I want you." I moved my hips, rubbing myself

against his hardness. His eyes fluttered closed, his head falling back against the sofa. "Admit you want me too," I murmured.

His eyes snapped open and locked onto mine. "I want you, Sky. Fuck I want you so bad right now."

My fingers dug into his broad shoulders as his lips collided with mine again. This kiss was harder than the last. It was a kiss fueled by pure desire. His hands slid down to cup my ass, pulling me against him, showing me what he was feeling.

My hips moved of their own accord, seeking relief. I rocked against his hard length, loving the way it felt pressed against my center.

Ben tore his mouth from mine and trailed his lips along my jaw, nibbling my ear lobe before moving down my neck. His hot mouth scorched a path as his lips and tongue and teeth explored the skin there. He pulled the strap of my dress aside, trailing his lips lower and lower.

"Oh, god, Ben," I moaned. I couldn't take it anymore. I started fiddling with his belt. "I need you," I panted, pulling his belt loose and working on the button of his jeans.

He grabbed my hand, halting my movements. "Wait."

"What?" I asked, confused. "Don't you want this?"

"Fuck yes, I want this. But not like this."

"I'm sorry, I'm pushing you too fast, aren't I?" I moved off his lap and sank into the couch beside him.

He stood up and grabbed my hand. "You aren't pushing anything. I just can't get you in the position I want you in on this couch." I let him tug me up and we rushed up the stairs to his bedroom. I had only been here a handful of times and they all involved helping him choose an outfit for some big meeting. To be here now, with Ben staring at me with lustful eyes, was a surreal experience I could barely even process. He gripped my waist, kissing me again.

I ran my hands up and down his chest, needing the barrier of his shirt to be removed. As if reading my thoughts, Ben ripped it off revealing his perfectly sculpted body. He spun me around and unzipped my dress with ease before slipping one strap over my shoulder. My left breast sprang loose and he groaned at the site of it.

"You look fucking incredible, Sky."

His hand cupped the bare mound and he tweaked my nipple, pinching it between his thumb and forefinger. A jolt of pleasure shot straight to my core. His hand left my breast and he slipped the other strap off my shoulder. The dress slid down my body, pooling at my feet. I was left in nothing but a tiny thong.

Ben took a step back and admired me. I stood there, letting him take his fill. His eyes devoured me, the hunger in them growing more and more. His gaze was so intense, I had to fight the urge to cover myself.

"You're the most beautiful woman I've ever seen," he said reverently.

"Ben," I breathed, his words sending a rush of heat through my body.

"Lie on the bed," he commanded.

I did as he said and propped myself up on my elbows.

"Take off your underwear," he demanded.

"So bossy," I said, obeying him.

"Isn't that appropriate?" he asked with a devilish grin.

My panties were off and I lay there completely bare. He crawled onto the bed, hovering above me before his mouth crashed down onto mine. His hand trailed my body, lingering on my stomach before descending lower.

"Oh!" I cried as soon as he reached the spot I'd been dying for him to touch. He circled his finger around my clit and I nearly lost my mind.

"You're so wet for me," he groaned.

I rocked against his hand, desperate for more friction. He plunged a finger inside and I nearly exploded. "Ben," I moaned.

"Fuck, hearing you say my name is going to be my undoing," he said.

"Please, Ben," I begged.

His fingers moved inside of me and I almost came undone right there. I moaned which just had him moving with more determination. His finger curled, hitting the perfect spot, and it was all over.

I cried out. My orgasm rocked through me, wave after wave crashing down. I'd never had an orgasm that powerful in my life.

"So responsive," he said, pulling his fingers out. "And so fucking tight," he murmured. He moved to his bedside drawer and pulled out a small foil packet. "I want to feel you wrapped around me."

"Yes, please," I breathed, reaching for him.

He moved back toward me, placing a knee on either

side of my legs. I wrapped a hand around his impressive length, stroking him a few times.

"Jesus, Sky," he groaned.

I stroked him a few more times and then guided him to my entrance. I was desperate for him to fill me. He pushed inside, filling me inch by inch until he was fully sheathed.

"You okay?" he asked.

"Mm hmm," I mumbled, unable to form words.

He slowly slid out and then pushed back in. His eyes rolled into the back of his head. "You feel amazing."

He picked up the pace, sliding in and out of me faster and harder. His body glistened with sweat. "God, I'm not going to last," he grunted.

He thrust into me hard and I gasped. Pleasure was building within me again. I needed him to go even deeper. Just when I thought I couldn't take anymore, his finger found my clit and rubbed hard.

"Oh!" I cried out, my legs beginning to tremble.

"Are you close?" he asked, his voice strained.

"Yes!"

"Come for me. I'm right behind you," he gritted out.

My release barreled through me. I cried out as the spasms racked my body.

Ben groaned. His eyes slammed shut and his hips bucked wildly. "God, I'm gonna—" He thrust once more and then went completely still, his mouth opening as he came. He collapsed on top of me and then quickly rolled us over so he was on his back, cradling me to his chest.

"That was incredible," he said.

I nodded in agreement, not yet able to speak. I couldn't even fathom that my biggest fantasy had just come true.

Benjamin Mead was mine.

We both drifted off into a deep, satisfied sleep.

Ben

DAY 14: FRIDAY

SUNLIGHT HIT MY FACE AS I LIFTED MY ARM ABOVE MY head and stretched. My muscles were sore from the night before and I smiled at the thought. I turned over to look at Skylar sleeping peacefully beside me. Last night had been absolutely incredible. Perhaps it wasn't the smartest idea to mix business and pleasure now that she'd be continuing to work for me, but I just couldn't resist her last night. She looked amazing in that dress and the way she stood up to my father had been my biggest turn-on to date. Plus, I'd be lying if I said I'd never thought about getting Skylar in my bed before.

It probably shouldn't happen again. It would just complicate things. No matter how much I'd like to claim her, I didn't deserve her. I'm sure Skylar would understand that. She didn't want to be having an affair with her boss. I'd say we could just keep things casual, but Sky deserved more than that. But as I stared at her still naked body, I had second thoughts. I already was thinking about grabbing her and making her scream my name again.

Before I could give in to my impulses, I slipped out of bed and threw on a T-shirt and sweatpants. I headed downstairs to start a pot of coffee.

Buddy greeted me as soon as I passed his bed in the living room. I ruffled his head before pouring a cup of food into his bowl.

I glanced at my phone left forgotten on the counter to see several texts from Nathan berating me for leaving the party early last night. As soon as I texted back with an apology, his name popped up on my screen as an incoming call.

"Where were you?" he barked.

"Relax, I had to step out. I did plenty of mingling before I left."

"You left me with those nightmares from the board."

"You're fine, Nathan," I said, suppressing the urge to roll my eyes. The guy was a genius, but his social ineptitude knew no bounds. "Why are you calling me other than to berate me?"

"I'm *only* calling to berate you," he grunted. "Where are you?"

I glanced at the clock on my stove. "It's only eight." Sure, I usually came into work at this time. But it was the Friday after an event. He could chill right the fuck out.

"Sky set up a few follow-up interviews for you this morning. One of the girls is already here."

"Tell her sorry for the late notice but the position has been filled."

"You found someone. Who?"

"Skylar," I said, a smile forming on my lips.

There was a long pause at the other end before Nathan finally said, "Are you sure? She seemed pretty committed to quitting."

"Not anymore. We worked it out."

Nathan sighed. "Fine, I'll get rid of her."

I hung up before he could say anything else negative to ruin my mood.

I sipped my coffee and pulled up my email, answering a few while I leaned against the kitchen island.

Footsteps padded against my wood floors and I looked up to see Skylar rounding the corner, wearing my sweatshirt. It was so big on her that it came down well past her mid-thigh. Possessiveness tugged at my chest at the sight of her in my clothes. I tried to shake the feeling. While she might be my employee, she wasn't mine to claim.

"Morning," she said, a hint of a blush creeping across her cheeks.

"Morning, beautiful."

I watched her walk towards me, unable to tear my eyes away from her curvy legs. My cock hardened immediately and I knew I was in trouble.

She stepped in between my legs and leaned forward, pressing a kiss to my lips. My eyebrows shot up in surprise at her forwardness. I gently grabbed her arm and forced her back a few inches. "Whoa there."

Her eyebrows knit in confusion. "Something wrong?"

"No, no, of course not." I shook my head. "Last night was...amazing."

She gave me a shy smile. "It was."

"But I think we should just keep it at that."

Her mouth hung open. "Excuse me?"

I scratched the back of my neck, hating these conversations. Surely, Skylar must see my point, though. "I'm still your boss, Sky. It could get messy. Fast."

Her eyes narrowed. "You're my boss for one more day. I hardly would call that messy."

My heart sank. "What do you mean? You said you'd stay?"

"What are you talking about?" She backed away from me, panic setting into her features. "I never said that."

"I told you I couldn't lose you. Then we came back here and...well you know." I waved my hand around, not wanting to bring up last night while she was staring at me like I was some sort of villain.

"I can't believe you." She shook her head in disbelief.

I took a step toward her but she moved all the way around the island to get away from me.

"You thought me sleeping with you last night was me agreeing to stay on?"

"Well, I thought when you said you didn't want to lose me either—"

"I wasn't talking about as a boss!" she exclaimed, cradling her face in her hands. "Oh no. Oh no. Oh no," she repeated. "I'm such an idiot. I can't believe I thought you wanted to be with me. I'm so stupid."

It felt like I got punched in the stomach. "I-I," I

gulped, trying to collect myself. "I just thought since you knew how I am…how I don't believe in relationships…I just thought you'd know that we didn't have a future." Saying those words made me feel like the world's biggest sleaze.

"Of course I thought we had a future!" she yelled. "You should have known I'd read into last night!"

She's right. What was wrong with me?

"I'm so sorry, Sky. I never meant to hurt you."

"Why the hell did you sleep with me then? You thought you'd what? Just fuck me and I'd go back to being your assistant?" she asked, her voice rising.

"No! That wasn't it at all!" I exclaimed. Maybe my actions last night hadn't been that of a rational man, but Skylar caused a lot of rational thoughts to leave me when she looked at me.

She crossed her arms and hung her head in defeat. "I thought when you said you couldn't lose me you meant as more than an assistant. I thought I meant more to you than that."

My heart cracked at her soft tone. "You do. But I can't ever offer you a commitment. You saw my dad last night—what a nightmare he is. That's the man that raised me. You know I could never be what you need."

She shook her head. "I actually don't know that. I know that's what you always tell yourself. I know that's how you keep people at a distance. But I thought—I thought I could be different."

I moved to reach for her again, but she held up her hands.

"You are different."

"No, I'm really not." She looked up with accusation in her eyes. "You knew how I felt about you. How could you be so cruel as to sleep with me, blow me off, and still think I'd be willing to work for you?"

I ran my hands over my face in frustration. What the hell *had* I been thinking? All I had known was that I wanted her—no needed her.

"Fuck, Sky, I don't know. You looked so perfect last night, and the way I had you on my arm…" I hesitated before continuing. "It was easy to forget that you weren't mine."

"But I could be," she said, tears streaming down her face. "I'm in love with you, Ben. You know I am."

Pain pierced through my chest at her hurt expression. I had to physically restrain myself from walking over to collect her in my arms and hold her until I saw her smile again.

Instead I just stood there like the biggest idiot on the planet. "I'm sorry. I don't know what I was thinking last night."

She shook her head slowly. "Goodbye, Ben. Consider my period of notice over. I'd rather die than go back into that office."

My heart cracked even though I had expected her to say that.

She moved silently toward the front door, not even going upstairs to collect the dress she wore yesterday.

"Let me drive you," I said weakly.

She glanced back one more time. "I'll call a cab. Frankly, I can't stand to be in the same space as you anymore."

I blew out a breath. "I'm sorry."

She shook her head slowly. "That's not enough anymore. Have a nice life."

With that she walked out of my house—and my life forever.

I DIDN'T DRAG MYSELF TO THE OFFICE THAT MORNING until noon. An unfamiliar heaviness sat on my chest, causing me to move at a glacial pace.

When I finally did walk to my office, the sight of her empty desk nearly made me turn around and never come back. How was I supposed to be here without her?

I moved through the door with my head down and slumped into my desk chair, spinning it around to look at the city below.

I felt fucking empty.

A knock on my doorframe was the only warning I had before Nathan walked in.

"The board decided to drop in today. They wanted to do lunch and I had to cover for you—again."

Nathan's curt tone already had my head throbbing.

"Oh," I said indifferently.

"What the hell is the matter with you?" he asked, walking around my desk so he could see my face.

"Sky quit after all," I muttered.

"So?"

He didn't get it and I couldn't explain it to him. He'd never understand what Sky meant to me.

Nathan let out a frustrated sigh. "You've seriously

got to stop lying to yourself. You know you're in love with her."

"I am not——"

"Don't try to deny it. Just think about it. You want her around all the time. You only want to talk to her. You couldn't let her go despite the multitude of skilled, beautiful women that came to interview for the position."

"I don't do love," I insisted.

"You need to figure your shit out, Ben. Your messy personal life is interfering with work and that's where I draw the line. Maybe your parents have given you a shit example of what a relationship should be, but that's no excuse to make yourself miserable."

My eyebrows drew together in confusion. Was this love? Was the reason I felt so sick right now because I just lost the only person I had ever felt anything for?

Nathan turned on his heel and walked out of my office. "Figure it out, Ben. I'm serious."

With that, he closed the door behind him, leaving my thoughts filled with nothing but the colossal mistake I had just made this morning.

Skylar

I JOTTED DOWN ANOTHER POTENTIAL ANSWER FOR AN interview question, but when I read it back it didn't make any sense. I could barely think over the blaring music in my headphones.

Groaning, I pulled my headphones off and looked over at Bria miserably. She had a textbook open but wasn't reading it. Instead she just glared at the kitchen wall.

"I'm going to murder them, I swear," she said.

Stanley and Stella were yelling at each other through the walls once again. Somehow, they seemed to have gotten even louder—although I'm not sure how that's possible.

"I'm going to bomb that final-round interview at this rate," I complained. "I can't even think straight." Maybe it was sad that I was spending my Saturday preparing for an interview on Monday, but I couldn't help it. I really wanted this job. I had nailed the first two conversations, and I really had a good feeling about this one. Best of all, my new boss would be a sweet woman in her sixties. No possibility of me falling hopelessly in love.

Bria put her hands over her ears and shook her head. "Well, I'm going to fail my test if they don't shut up."

Someone knocked at the door and I scanned my brain, trying to remember if we had ordered that pizza we talked about.

Bria shot up and walked toward the door. She swung it open and slammed it shut before I even had a chance to peek outside.

"Oh hell no!" she exclaimed. "Get out of here."

I sprang up and raced to her side. "Who is it?"

"It's me." The muffled voice sent a shiver down my spine.

"Like I said, get out of here," Bria yelled again.

"Sky, please just give me two minutes."

I shook my head, heat rising to my cheeks. "Please leave, Ben. I said everything I had to say yesterday."

"Well I didn't," he said.

Bria rolled her eyes and swung the door open. "If you had something to say to Skylar you should have said it yesterday. She's done with you. Forever."

He stood there looking completely dejected and holding a cardboard box. He didn't even look at Bria, instead his eyes pleaded with mine. Despite all the tears I already cried over him yesterday, more threatened to spill out at the mere sight of him.

Bria went to close the door on him again, but he put his foot in the way and shoved himself inside.

"Hey!" she exclaimed. "This is breaking and entering!"

I shook my head, between the yelling next door and the yelling in here, I was completely overwhelmed.

Ben took two steps toward me, but I backed away quickly.

"What do you want?" I demanded.

"I just want to talk, please."

Bria folded her arms across her chest. "What could you possibly have to say? Come here to give Skylar more bullshit reasons why you treated her the way that you did? Well she doesn't need them."

Ben moved the box he was holding to the side and positioned it under one arm. With his other hand, he pinched the bridge of his nose.

At that moment, a loud clatter came from next door.

"Can we go outside to talk," he begged, pretending like Bria wasn't still berating him.

"She's not going anywhere with you."

I sighed and shook my head. "Let me just hear him out."

Bria groaned and glared between the two of us. "Fine. Make your own mistakes. See if I care." She pointed at me. "But no more crying to me when he inevitably upsets you again."

"That's not going to happen," Ben said, eyes still trained on me.

I pulled down the sleeves of my worn gray sweatshirt and breezed past Ben. I walked out our door and took the stairs two at a time until I was out on the sidewalk in front of our building.

He followed closely on my heels. When I finally turned around to face him, I felt a little justified seeing how anxious he appeared to be.

His eyebrows narrowed in concern. "Your neighbors are really out of control."

I shrugged. "Tell me something I don't know."

"You really shouldn't be living in a place like this—"

I held up my hand. "I get it. You think I live in a bad neighborhood."

He winced, looking up and down the street. "I wouldn't say bad. I just hate thinking of you here by yourself."

"I have Bria," I reminded him.

"Still. I don't like it at all."

I folded my arms across my chest. "Well it's a good thing my wellbeing is none of your business."

His jaw tensed. "That's where you're wrong."

Raising my eyebrows, I tilted my head. "Excuse me?"

I wasn't over what had happened yesterday morning. Not even close. I had already accepted that I'd likely never see Ben again. Yet here he was, tracking me down at my apartment. Looking as amazing as ever, albeit a little flustered.

"Shit I'm already messing this up," he muttered, before holding out the box he carried. "You didn't stop by to get your things from the office."

I sucked in a breath. Was that all this was?

"I couldn't face you," I admitted.

"And that kills me. It kills me even more that it's my fault," he said before holding up a stuffed animal.

"Remember when an advertising company sent this? I was going to throw it away and you begged to keep it. You said it was too cute to have such a grim fate."

I shrugged, pretending I didn't remember. "You can give it to your new dog. Looks like a good chew toy."

He dropped the stuffed toy back in the box and retrieved a neon orange stress ball. "Remember when you'd throw this at me any time I'd make a dirty joke? You told me you were training me with negative reinforcement."

"I barely remember that."

"That's because I've hardly made a dirty joke in years." He smirked. "Your training worked wonders."

"Is there a point to this?" I asked, trying not to let my heart be swayed by whatever this strange gesture was.

Ben ignored me and pulled out a sweater. "Remember when I bought you this? You complained every morning about how cold it was in the office, yet you still showed up every day in short sleeves." He smiled. "You were so stubborn."

"It *was* too cold in there," I insisted. "Why should I dress to accommodate inhumane working conditions."

A twinkle appeared in his eye as he shook his head.

He rummaged through the box before pulling out a framed picture of the two of us. It was just a silly selfie we took when I first started.

"Remember when you told me it was too sad that I didn't have any pictures in my office? You printed and framed this the next day."

"I remember," I murmured, thinking back as if it were yesterday.

He nodded, setting down the box at his feet and stepping around it. I backed up instinctively, and I couldn't help but notice the hurt in his eyes.

"I miss you terribly," he said.

"It's been one day," I whispered, my breath catching in my throat.

"One miserable, awful day where I thought of nothing but you and how much of an asshole I am."

My gaze drifted to the floor as tears built behind my eyes. "It's whatever, Ben. It's over—"

"No it's not," he said forcefully. He reached out and gripped my arms, causing me to look up at him. His eyes searched mine.

"I'm so sorry about yesterday. I can't apologize enough. I should have been on my knees begging you to be mine."

His last words made my heart skip. Did I hear him right or had all my fantasies officially caused me to start hallucinating?

My mouth opened and closed. He had rendered me completely speechless.

He took the opportunity to tuck a piece of hair behind my ear and take my chin between his index finger and thumb before tilting my face up toward his.

"I'm such an idiot. I've spent my whole life telling myself I'd never end up miserable like my parents. They've done nothing but cheat on each other and prove to me love doesn't exist." I gulped as he leaned into me further. "But in my quest to not be like them,

I've ended up miserable in a completely different way. I was too blind to even realize what falling for someone felt like. Instead of leaning into it, I pushed it away. But I can't do that anymore. I can't lose you. I only cared about you being my assistant because I needed you in my life and I wasn't sure how to keep you. But I'm in love with you, Sky. I should have recognized it a hell of a lot sooner, but I didn't. I'm sorry for that. But I'm hoping to god that you'll give me another chance because I meant it when I said I couldn't lose you."

Tears were full on streaming down my face now. He used his other thumb to brush them away.

"That's everything I ever wanted to hear," I stammered, my voice weak. "But yesterday—after everything that happened—it made me realize something."

Concern flashed across his face. "What did it make you realize?"

I sighed. "That if I let you in and you leave…I'll be completely ruined. My heart will shatter even more than I thought possible."

Ben cupped my cheeks in his hands and gazed down at me intensely. "I won't be leaving. You can bet on that."

"Ben—"

"Trust me, Sky. I can't leave you. This whole time I've been in an absolute state of panic at the thought of you quitting. I thought it was because I couldn't lose you as an assistant. That was fucking dumb of me. I should have realized it was because I physically can't go on without you. I just didn't piece that together until it was too late."

My breath hitched.

"You own me, okay? I've done nothing for the past twenty-four hours except wallow and make lists of how I'll make this up to you. Trust me, I'm already completely shattered without you."

I stood there still silent. It was everything I'd ever dreamed of hearing, but the shock of it all had my brain temporarily frozen.

Ben's eyes pleaded with mine. "Please tell me you still love me and I'll spend every day proving to you that you're the only girl for me."

I bit my lip and nodded.

Relief flooded his features. "I need to hear you say it."

"I'll always love you," I whispered.

Before the words had fully left my mouth, his lips were on mine. Kissing me with urgency. After a few minutes he broke free, before kissing my forehead.

He held me around my waist before looking back at my apartment building.

"So, now that this is out of the way, can I steal you away to come live with me? I really can't think about the love of my life living here."

Ben

"Can you believe it's the ten-month anniversary of our first kiss?" I asked, handing Skylar a box of Chinese takeout. She sat curled up next to me on the couch we'd purchased together. After she moved in, I wanted her to feel like the space was just as much hers as it was mine.

"I can't believe you remember that," she said, digging her chopsticks into the box.

I chuckled. "Of course I remember that. I thought about it nonstop after it happened."

She ducked her chin and rolled her eyes. Buddy pawed over and sat beneath her, begging for a scrap of food.

"I think I was the one doing all the fantasizing," she said.

Grinning, I took another bite. "Trust me, I did plenty of fantasizing. I just didn't tell you about it."

The past six months had been absolute bliss. I couldn't believe I had almost denied myself the pleasure of being in love with Skylar. This was the first time in my life I had ever felt truly happy. Not only was I successful, but I also had someone to share it with.

"The board finally made that decision about the merger," I said carefully. While Skylar and I were still in the honeymoon phase of our relationship, there had been a bit of a sticking point recently. There was a chance Pulse needed me to move to Denver for a new acquisition. Skylar wasn't keen on leaving her new job, and I completely understood. She was killing it there and had already moved up to a director of communication position. But at the same time, I was obligated to move to Denver for my company, and leaving her behind was absolutely not an option.

"What did they say?" Skylar asked, leaning her head back against the couch, looking tired.

"The move is definite," I said.

She groaned. "I knew you were going to say that. What are we going to do?"

"I know you don't want to leave your job," I started.

She nodded. "I mean that's part of it for sure. I know I can get another job, but it all feels so fast." She gestured around the house. "You convinced me to move in with you basically immediately."

"That apartment wasn't safe," I insisted.

Skylar had tried to resist me, but it only took a few weeks of my constant begging before she moved in with me. I think Bria had been the one to actually convince her, though. Because I couldn't stand her being there alone, I slept over every night. Bria said we needed to get the hell out of there before our happiness made her physically sick.

Skylar waved off my concern. "Whatever. It was still fast. And now moving to a new city with you?" She bit her lip.

"I love you," I said simply.

"I love you too, but aren't you nervous we're rushing things?"

The bulge in my back pocket suddenly felt molten hot.

"I don't," I said, reaching for it.

"What if you get sick of me," she groaned. "I really can't take that."

"I won't get sick of you." I smirked down at her.

"I don't know, maybe we should slow things down. You could move out there, we can do the long distance, and then I can follow if everything goes well."

I chuckled. "I'm absolutely not doing that."

She sighed. "Well, what do you suggest then?"

"This," I said, slipping off the couch and dropping to one knee in front of her.

Her mouth hung open in shock.

"Skylar, I love you so much. I would argue that we're not rushing because I took my sweet-ass time recognizing what we had. I want to make up for all that lost time I spent being an idiot and pushing you away. Don't move to Denver as my girlfriend, move there as my wife."

My heart beat rapidly as tears streamed down her face. She silently stared at the ring and then back to me.

After a few seconds, I let out the breath I had been holding. "Is that a yes, or…?"

"Yes!" she exclaimed, flinging herself into my arms. "Yes, a thousand times."

Relief and happiness coursed through my veins. I slid the ring I had carefully picked out on her finger and kissed her forehead.

For someone who thought they didn't deserve love, I had never been happier to be proven wrong.

The End

<u>Love Linked, Nathan's Story, out now!</u>

After a reluctant move to Denver, Nathan meets Charlie. She's bold, intelligent and—unlike the other employees —she isn't afraid to stand up to him. Although he's never been able to connect with people in the past— something about her makes him want to try...

Read it now or flip through for a sneak peek!

Nathan

THE SLEEK GLASS WALLS OF OUR SAN DIEGO OFFICE overlooked the bustling city below. I moved from the window to sit behind my desk—my posture rigid, fingers tapping an urgent rhythm against the polished wood. I normally found comfort in the pristine space I had created—a reflection of my own meticulous nature.

But right now it felt stifling.

"Moving our entire office to Denver? You can't be serious." I shot an accusatory look across the room to Ben, my business partner, cofounder, and former college roommate.

"It's where Love Linked is located, and they finalized the merger yesterday. It's a done deal, Nathan. We knew we'd be giving up control when we took on these investors."

"But not that much control," I seethed. "Our entire company that we built from the ground up is being merged with some up-and-coming app and we get no say?"

Love Linked, the small dating app our investors had recently acquired in Denver, was the exact opposite of our app, Pulse. It championed genuine connections and meaningful relationships over the casual encounters people usually sought our services for.

"That up-and-coming app has been getting a hell of a lot of press lately. Their growth numbers are off the charts. Besides…" Ben's typical charisma—usually used to charm the board—had vanished. Instead, he flashed me a sheepish grin. "They want us to clean up our image."

"The image *you* fostered," I said, my eyes narrowing in accusation.

Despite our completely dissimilar personalities, our collaboration had birthed a multi-million-dollar dating application used by millions all over the world. While we had started with good intentions in college—just trying to connect like-minded people so they could build a real connection—our venture had, over time, transformed from that innocent concept into a sophisticated yet sleazy platform. Some people might not like to point fingers, but I had no issue with it. Our image was entirely Ben's fault, likely due to his notorious former playboy nature.

Ben held up his hands in defense and leaned back in his chair. "Oh, now that it's a problem it's *my* image? You didn't seem to take issue with it when we raked in our first million dollars."

I scowled at his deflection. "I always told you we should tone it down, and you fought me tooth and nail on it. You're only on board with it now because you're in a relationship. The old you would have never stood for it."

He rolled his eyes. "Alright, calm down. So what if I fell in love? It didn't change my business savviness. At the time, I thought playing up the sex made the most sense. But now, I can see the appeal of having a softer side."

"That's what I've always said." I let out a frustrated groan. "Now that we've finally brought on investors, it's the first thing they want to fix. Just like I told you."

He raised his eyebrows. "You're really going to go with the 'I told you so' route? So cliché."

"I am and I did," I insisted, irritated by his relaxed attitude. This company was everything to me. To have this level of control ripped away in a matter of weeks infuriated me. When we signed this deal, it felt too good to be true. Almost as if we were signing our souls away to the devil for a billion dollars. Now we had to pay the price.

Ben shook his head. "I don't know why you're so upset about this then. We're finally taking this app in the direction you wanted."

"Under someone else's demand!"

"No need to raise your voice," Ben said, holding up his hands. "What's done is done. We'll send out the announcement to the office on Monday. A few will be given the option to relocate, but most will be able to stay on remotely. You and I need to be in Denver for this, end of story. We'll be leading the merger and the integration of both apps into one new product."

I gripped my desk, hating to concede but knowing fighting was futile.

"When are we leaving?" I finally asked.

"Next week." He blew out a breath, knowing the worst of our conversation had ended.

"Just like that?"

He shrugged. "Just like that."

I stuffed my hands into the pockets of my stiff, expensive jeans and stared out at the expansive city view. "But the winter." I winced at the thought.

Ben chuckled. "A little cold could do you some good. Haven't you seen those guys that do ice baths for their health? It's supposed to make you superhuman or something."

I sighed. The prospect of relocating didn't inherently upset me. California had been my residence ever since I ventured out here for college. While I wasn't eager to vacate, it also never felt quite like home. Likely due to the loner status I embraced.

My reservations stemmed from the principle of the matter. That my life was being dictated by outside forces, despite my full capability of making all major company decisions.

When I turned around, Ben's hopeful expression stopped me dead in my tracks. As much as it killed me, the realist in me couldn't deny this plan made a lot of sense. Our growth numbers had been dwindling, and this merger was likely our ticket to branching out into a new market.

"I'll start looking for a place," I relented.

Ben whistled and looked up at the ceiling. "Thank

god that's over. Honestly, you took that better than I expected."

I glared at him in response.

"Hey, isn't your brother out in Denver?" Ben asked.

Stiffening, I tilted my head so he couldn't see my face. "Your point?"

"Won't it be nice being close to family?"

"Oliver and I don't exactly have a lot in common." That was the understatement of the century. Where people often viewed me as cold and uptight, they saw Oliver as the fun-loving brother with an easygoing attitude and a zest for life. I wouldn't say I envied him, but it had always bothered me the way he never let anything get to him—the way he always put his enjoyment for life and adventure above all else.

Where was his sense of responsibility? His work ethic?

While I went off to college, he moved to Colorado to be a snowboard instructor. Then he was a rafting guide. Then a rock-climbing teacher.

I couldn't keep up with what he was doing nowadays.

"Well, family is family. And, let's face it, your social roster is pretty much nonexistent here, Nathan."

"I'll call him," I said, already dreading the forced obligation.

Ben got up from his seat and walked around my desk to smack me on the shoulder. "This is going to be a good chapter. I can feel it."

Charlie

"NATHAN SHAW AND BEN MEAD FROM PULSE WILL BE arriving next week to handle the merger. Any questions?" Don, our CEO, addressed us all as we stood in a large semi-circle around him. He had just finished dropping the bomb that we'd be merging with the sex-crazed dating app.

My hand shot up in the air, and he eyed it disdainfully. "Yes, Charlie?"

"We're on track to grow three hundred percent this year. Why would we merge with an outdated sexist app that could drag down our numbers?"

Murmurs erupted around the room.

Don chuckled in that crude way he always did. I resisted the urge to scrunch my nose in disgust while he eyed me.

"Always so blunt, aren't you Charlie?" He shook his head and made a tsking sound as if scolding me like a child. A hand pinched my arm, and I knew without looking that Lila stood next to me. "Pulse is still the number one dating app in the country. We'll grow exponentially by merely associating ourselves with them. Plus, we could use the sex appeal."

"Is that really going to appeal to our target audience?" I challenged.

"It appeals to everyone." He winked at me, and I had to physically restrain myself from gagging. "Make sure you don't ask these questions to Nathan and Ben when they arrive. We want to make sure we're welcoming. Obviously, as the director of product you'll be leading this merger on our end."

Great. Just what I wanted—to be thrown into the lion's den.

When I joined Love Linked in its infancy, the concept drew me in. A dating app that focused on meaningful questions and finding real connections. Now that I had been here five years, it had lost virtually all of its appeal. Largely due to the owner, Don, being an absolute sexist prick. I should have known it on my first day when he said that we had to come up with more thoughtful "dumbass questions to lure in desperate women." Oh, the irony, of a dating app aimed to attract women being run by the biggest misogynist I had ever met.

And now, it seemed, two more just like him would be joining the ranks. I highly doubted the owners of Pulse would do anything to maintain the integrity the rest of the staff had painstakingly cultivated at Love Linked.

"This is unbelievable," I whispered to Lila.

She glanced at me and gave a sympathetic wince. This integration was about to be hell.

I pretended to listen as Don droned on about insignificant details before finally releasing us. Lila followed me to my desk and leaned over my divider.

Even though I had worked hard and held a high position at this company, only Don had his own office. Well, I guess Nathan and Ben would have one now too.

"I can't believe Nathan Shaw and Ben Mead are going to be here next week," Lila, my best friend and head of our design team, whisper-squealed.

Furrowing my eyebrows, I sat back in my seat. "You act like that's something to be excited about."

"Are you kidding?" She brushed her rust-colored hair over her shoulder and looked dreamily off into the distance. "This is by far the most exciting thing that has happened at this company in years."

"I wouldn't go that far. Remember last year when Don almost had that sexual harassment lawsuit go to court?"

She waved off my dry tone. "Seriously, Charlie, think about it. Nathan and Ben are practically celebrities in the tech world and they'll be here. In *this* office. In *our* meetings."

I wasn't impressed, despite her best efforts. "Aren't they supposed to be big playboys? I remember reading some articles about it."

"So? That only adds to the drama." She rubbed her hands together.

I shook my head. "All it's adding to is the number of misogynistic assholes in charge around here."

"At least these misogynistic assholes are hot," Lila said, holding out her phone. "I mean have you seen their pictures? That alone should get you a little excited."

I didn't even bother glancing up as I opened my laptop to send out a few emails. "I swear, if I didn't know better, I'd say you thrived in this toxic work environment."

Lila rolled her large green eyes. "You know I don't." She leaned in further and whispered so that only I could hear. "Hopefully, the two of us won't be here for much longer. It'll be kind of fun to sit back and watch what happens."

"Lila," I hissed, whipping my head around to ensure no one heard. "No talking about that in the office."

"Relax. No one is paying attention to us. Everyone's still busy over there sucking up to Don."

I glanced back to see all the male department heads cackling at some no-doubt tasteless joke Don had cracked.

Groaning, I averted my eyes. "This place is hell," I muttered.

"But it won't be ours for much longer," Lila sing songed. I hushed her again and shooed her away.

Read Love Linked now!

About the Author

Allison Speka is a long-time reader of romance. She met her partner in Chicago before they both picked up and moved to Colorado six years ago.

Follow along on her publishing journey @SpekaAllison on TikTok or @allisonspeka on Instagram!

Made in the USA
Middletown, DE
18 September 2024